ALIEN DOMINATION

TAUREAN WARRIORS SERIES

MELODY BECKETT

Alien Domination: Taurean Warriors Series by Melody Beckett

Published by Bronzewing Books

Copyright © 2022 Melody Beckett

www.melodybeckett.com

For permissions contact: hello@melodybeckett.com

Cover by Kasmit Covers

Editing by Write Now Creative

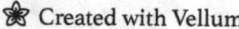 Created with Vellum

For those who are trying to accept their pasts so they can move into the future.

CONTENT NOTES

This book touches on some topics that may be sensitive for some readers. These include: battles with aliens, building collapse, being captured and imprisoned, mentions of parental and grandparental death, abandonment as a child, and claustrophobia. Alien Domination also includes explicit language and sex scenes.

Reading is something we do as an escape, so if you think this book may be uncomfortable for you to read then please feel free to skip.

Happy reading,

Mel xx

ALIEN DOMINATION

CHAPTER ONE

Domik

E arth. The planet he'd heard so much about spun peacefully below them, Domik transfixed as he watched through the small window of the shuttle's galley. He could see why CJ spoke so fondly of her home planet. It was beautiful.

He turned his attention to the woman in question, sitting across from him at the small table. Sergeant Clodagh Jones of Earth's Space Force. Battlefield medic and the only woman Domik had ever felt more than a passing interest in. A mere slip of a woman compared to Domik, who stood almost eight feet tall, but what she lacked in size she made up for in attitude. And, in the year that he'd known her, his feelings for her had grown from mere interest to raging inferno.

He had tried fighting his feelings, to no avail. His limited experience with women—human or otherwise—had him questioning every interaction with her, no matter how small, until the only thing he was certain of was that she tolerated his company.

But he wanted more. So much more. If only he could be certain that she returned his feelings.

He watched her, committing every small movement to memory to play back later when he was alone. She was so cute when her face screwed up in concentration when they played chess, oblivious to Domik's stare. A small frown line divided her delicately arched blond eyebrows, her chin propped on her hand as she stared at the pieces on the board in front of her.

And... there it was. Like a lightning bolt, desire shot through him. Domik shifted in his seat, his knee banging on the underside of the table and drawing a sharp look from CJ as the pieces on the chessboard wobbled.

"Sorry," he said.

Domik was notorious for being calm, and his own brother had even called him unemotional on more than one occasion. But not around CJ. She got under his skin—had captivated him, body and soul. And Domik had no idea what to do about it.

His lips thinned into a line as he fought against what was now a familiar, and frustrating, sense of uncertainty. Until he had met CJ, he had always known what to do. His childhood had been filled with advanced classes, then tutors, until he had exceeded the ability of even the most knowledgeable of his teachers. His parents enrolled him at the best Taurean university, but he had been so much younger than the other students that he had nothing in common with them.

Loneliness had become expected. He had spent most of his life surrounded by people who didn't understand him.

And he'd never had a sexual encounter that lasted longer than one night, let alone an actual relationship. He was attracted to women, sure, but he did not know how to even begin when he had feelings for someone. Let alone the passion he held for CJ. So he had defaulted to being her friend. And now he was stuck, afraid to ask for more lest he lose her completely.

Domik sighed, crossing his arms over his chest. It was quiet in the galley. The only sounds were the gentle hum of the engines and the distant conversation of Zac, Laila, T'arq and Krystal who were in the cockpit just down the hall. The small eating area where they sat was the only common area in the shuttle—the only place with a table to set up a chess set—and the spot where CJ and Domik waged war.

Domik had lost count of how many games they had played over the past few months. They had played one day on the Starship Zataras, shortly after the Taureans and humans had joined forces against the evil insectoid Xakul race. CJ had traded for it with another human, as happened when luxury items were in short supply, and it had become their thing.

Warmth flooded his chest as he watched the slender human deliberate over her next move. He had learnt so much about her playing this game. She was naturally quite cautious, often taking a long time to decide on her move, but once she decided, she stuck to it. Like now. There was only one move she could make and still have a chance of winning. Domik had planned it that way, and in hindsight, it would have been easier to just win. Losing at chess on purpose was much harder than winning. Especially when his opponent wasn't actually any good at the game. Or any game of strategy.

3

But he didn't care about winning. At least not against her.

She lifted her head from her hand and pursed her lips as she moved her rook, sitting back in her seat and crossing her arms over her chest. She lifted her chin, her hazel eyes flashing a challenge as they met his. Her high cheekbones, pointed chin, and the way she kept her mop of blond hair cropped short gave her an almost ethereal appearance. But looks could be deceiving. She might look fragile, but she was far from it, even though she sometimes didn't believe that herself.

Domik scowled in mock thought as he gazed at the chessboard on the table in front of him. In reality, he'd decided what move to make within seconds of CJ moving her rook, but he treasured these quiet moments they shared.

The hum of the shuttle's engine was the only sound in the small galley, apart from their breathing. And the quiet tapping of CJ's short nails on the polished metal tabletop. The walls were the same dull gray color of the Taurean fleet vessels, though the cushions that padded the benches were bright purple. Domik had wondered at that, and T'arq, who was the shuttle's pilot, had just laughed when he'd asked about it. The table where they sat was bolted to the floor and around it were bench seats in a U shape. On the opposite wall to the table was a bench with a replication machine to make food and storage cupboards. All in all, it was a pretty standard shuttle.

Tap. Tap tap. Tap. CJ's nails drummed an impatient beat.

Domik forced himself to not smile. He never smiled. But lately it had been harder and harder to maintain his stoic facade. At least around CJ.

Domik lifted his hand from the edge of the table, letting it hover over the chessboard as if in hesitation. The tapping of CJ's nails ceased, and Domik flicked a look toward her, his dark, almost black, eyes taking in the bright hazel of hers for a long moment, before looking back at the chessboard. He pressed his lips into a thin line, hand still hovering over the board, before his deep bronze fingers reached slowly toward one of his pieces.

A slight gasp from CJ stayed his hand, and Domik pressed his lips tighter together to stop the grin that was bursting to spread across his face. He picked up the knight and moved it into place. She would have no option but to declare check now.

"Honestly, Domik. You'd think that after all these months of me teaching you how to play that you wouldn't get caught like this anymore." CJ's voice was a light trill across his skin. Her words, even exasperated as they were, sending waves of pleasure through him. He barely managed a non-committal mumble in reply. "Check," she said with a triumphant grin.

He watched as she sat back in on the bench seat opposite him, arms crossed over the dark gray of her flight suit, as she waited for him to make his move. Her short, white-blond hair sticking up at odd angles where earlier she had run her hands through it. He'd learnt she called the style a pixie cut, though Domik did not know what a mythical human creature had to do with hair. Her lips, a pale pink he found fascinating compared to the bronze of his own, quirked as she winked at him.

"C'mon, big guy. Show me what you've got."

Domik's eyes widened slightly at that. Surely she didn't—

"Oh! Not like that," she said, her smile dropping as she waved a hand at the chessboard. "Your next move."

Domik shifted slightly on the seat. He had shown no sign of his thoughts, and yet she had known. This was not good.

CJ cleared her throat and looked away, rubbing her arms as if cold, and swallowing. Domik dropped his hand to adjust the rather uncomfortable bulge that had grown at the mention of showing her—but no. Not going there. She wouldn't be interested. She was all sunshine and brightness, while he was the exact opposite.

Enough women had propositioned him over the years for him to know how they saw him. All they saw was his colossal size and wanted to see what he was like in bed. And when he had an itch, he scratched it. But it never satisfied the deep ache in his chest. Domik craved a connection with one person—one soul—that went beyond just a physical encounter. He wanted to be loved. By her.

Sighing, he lifted his hand and moved one of the pieces on the board.

CJ darted a glance at him from the piece he'd just moved to his face and back. "Are you sure you want to move that one?"

Domik shrugged as if it was of no consequence.

She gave him one last look before breaking into a grin. "Check mate!" she cried, dragging her plump pink lip between her teeth and making the move that ended the game. "You really should practice more, Domik." Her eyes sparkled with humor as she sat back, lifting one eyebrow, her lips quirking.

Domik just shrugged, pushing away from the table to slide out into the cramped walkway that ran through the galley. Big, even for a Taurean warrior, Domik had to contort himself just to get out of the space, his leg banging against

CJ's under the table. His skin burned from the touch, and he froze.

"Did I hurt you?" he asked, pausing as he waited for her answer, stomach lurching at the thought he might have caused her some pain, no matter how small.

"Nope, big guy. I'm fine," she replied, pulling her legs up onto the bench seat so he could move a little easier. "You do you." She waved her hand in the general direction of his legs.

Domik slid free and stood, stretching his arms over his head to brace against the ceiling of the galley. Sitting in such a cramped position had him needing to stretch. His muscles becoming stiff from lack of movement. As he moved, his tee-shirt pulled free from the waistband of his combat trousers, sliding up over his stomach. A gasp had him frozen in place, looking down at the woman, who was staring up at him intently.

"Is something wrong?" he asked, eyebrows knitting in confusion.

CJ mumbled something under her breath, slipping with enviable ease from her side of the table to stand in front of him. She reached up and tugged at the hem of his black tee-shirt, her fingers brushing briefly against his taught stomach in a delicate caress.

Domik's breath caught, his abdominal muscles clenching at her whisper light touch. He froze, hands above his head, looking down at where her fingers were still tugging at his shirt.

"Don't they make clothes big enough for you?" She asked through gritted teeth, as she tried to cover the sliver of exposed bronzed skin.

Domik let his arms drop, the shirt's hem sliding back into

place, his brows knitted in confusion. There was nothing wrong with his clothes. Sure, the shirts he wore were the biggest available, and they pulled tight across his shoulders and chest, but there wasn't anything he could do about that. CJ gave a small harrumph and stepped back, not meeting his eyes. A slight blush coloring her cheeks.

A metallic whoosh had both of them turning to watch the galley door slide open, and Commander Zac Qu'Rell stepped through, Domik taking a step backward and CJ shuffling her feet. The battle-scarred Taurean warrior gave them an assessing look before turning to the replicator and pressing a series of buttons.

Turning his back to the machine, he leaned against the wall, arms crossed over his chest. One side of his face was badly scarred, giving him a sinister appearance, his bulky size only adding to that impression. He wasn't as tall as Domik, but Zac had bested him enough on the wrestling mats to know that wasn't all that mattered. The much-respected commander raised an eyebrow and looked pointedly at Domik and CJ, the silence in the galley stretching uncomfortably.

Domik, realizing he was still standing in the same spot, turned and tidied the chess set back into its box.

"Who won this time?" Zac asked.

CJ laughed, sounding forced to Domik's ears. "I did. Again. Didn't I, big guy?" She smiled up at him before turning to Zac. "Do you need me back on the bridge?"

Zac nodded. "Yes. It's almost time."

CJ's formerly jovial expression dropped, replaced with what Domik thought of as her battle-ready face. "Right. Back to it then." She left the room, the door sliding shut behind her.

Zac turned to Domik. "You're still letting her win?"

Domik didn't reply, shifting the chess set from one hand to the other.

The replicator beeped and Zac turned, pulling two steaming mugs of what smelled like coffee from the machine. "You should tell her how you feel."

The only sign that Domik had heard the words of his commander was a slight tensing of his shoulders.

"You know I'm right." Zac titled his head toward the doorway. "She likes you."

"Like." Domik snorted and shook his head. "It's not enough."

But doesn't she play chess with you almost every day? It could be a start.

It wasn't as if there was a lot of choice of company when they were on a mission. Almost everyone else was part of a couple, except for CJ and Domik. It made sense that they would spend time together. Domik strode from the galley, turning down the hallway away from the bridge, his steps fast as if he could escape his own thoughts.

The shuttle was not the smallest vessel he'd worked on, but it wasn't far from it. Aside from the galley, where they would replicate food and drinks, there was the bridge and a small medical bay. The white space was currently empty, ready for any injured or sick crew member. It was not a long-term treatment facility, as the ship was only used for short reconnaissance missions with a small crew.

Domik continued down the hallway, passing the room that

served as sleeping quarters. The tiny space was packed with two sets of bunk beds so close together that Domik's broad shoulders got jammed in between them if he tried to turn around.

A few more steps and he was in the cargo hold. It was barely large enough to lay claim to the name, and it was Domik's personal domain. He swiped his wrist against the scanner pad next to the door, which opened with a blast of frigid air. They kept the cargo hold much cooler than the rest of the ship, on account of the plasma bombs that currently took up a significant amount of the available space.

As the weapons specialist, he maintained and used every weapon on this ship. The plasma bombs were Domik's own personal prototype, changed from the standard Taurean design, and ready to be deployed in the war against the Xakul. In fact, most of the weapons used by the Taurean military were either designed or modified by Domik.

He strode into the space, pulling a tablet from the pocket on the side of his combat trousers and flicking through the screens until he found the one he was after. A quick survey of the bombs reassured him they were all in good condition, having suffered no ill effects of the transit from the Zataras' armory to the shuttle.

Domik quickly got to work, loading the bombs into their chutes next to the cargo hold, and readying them for use.

A beeping from the comm unit strapped to his wrist had Domik stopping in his work. He flicked his hand, activating the channel. "Yes?"

Zac's voice filled the space. "Domik, to the bridge. Now."

The urgency in his commander's voice had Domik replying that he'd be there as soon as he could. Finishing his task quickly, he strode down the hallways and to the bridge.

The door opened as he approached, no need to swipe his wrist this time. Casting a look around the space, he saw their pilot T'arq and his flight engineer, Krystal, heads close together as they poured over what looked like a 3D map projected up from the viewscreen in front of them. The pair had recently moved into couple's quarters on the Zataras, the previously wild T'arq showing a different side now that he had settled down with Krystal. The two sat in the pilot and co-pilot's seats to the front of the bridge and immediately before a gigantic wall of glass that was currently showing a view of the humans' home planet and its single moon.

Domik found it amusing that the humans had called their moon just that. Moon.

He looked to the right of the bridge where Zac and Laila were looking at a tablet together, their heads almost touching as they whispered. Zac looked up at Domik's arrival, passing the tablet to Laila and giving a small smile. The skin on the left side of Zac's face pulled slightly with the movement of his lips, the scarring he had incurred during battle with the Xakul crisscrossing his face and neck. Domik had seen Zac sparring shirtless and knew the scars carried down his torso and arm as well. He had been lucky to survive his wounds.

Luckier still to find a woman who loved him just the way he was in Laila. The former captain in Earth's Space Force rested a hand on Zac's scarred arm, giving a gentle squeeze before moving to her own seat.

"Good. You're here," Zac said, waving a hand toward Domik's station where he would manage the ship's weapons throughout the upcoming battle. "Everyone, there have been some... developments."

CJ spun around in her chair at the communications

station. When not required for her medic skills, she doubled as a communications specialist, acting as a go-between with the Zataras. "What developments?" she asked in a deceptively even voice.

Domik settled into his seat next to her, flicking a hand over the screen to arrange it to his specifications.

Zac continued. "The Xakul attack is imminent. Likely within the next hour."

Domik looked at the faces of the people he knew as friends. The only ones missing were his brother, Oren, and the human doctor that Oren was... well, Domik wasn't exactly sure what Oren and Amelia were to each other, but they were close. Oren was currently on a mission elsewhere, his role with Taurean intelligence taking him away from this battle. Amelia, being one of the few medical doctors familiar with human anatomy, was on the Zataras, readying the medical team for casualties.

"Zac, we knew that already. What's the news?" Krystal's soft voice was in contrast to CJ's more abrasive and demanding tones. T'arq's hand came to rest on Krystal's, winding his fingers between hers and squeezing gently.

Zac took a deep breath. "The rest of the Taurean fleet is not coming."

Domik straightened in his seat. That was not good news.

"Why?" This time it was T'arq who asked the question.

"There was a terrorist attack by the Taurean Purists. The details are hazy, but there's enough damage to delay them, and perhaps to prevent them from coming at all. We can't count on reinforcements." Zac paused, looking around at the stunned group.

"Does that seem a little too much of a coincidence to anyone else?" T'arq asked, Domik nodding his agreement.

It didn't matter though, not really. What mattered was the here and now. The Xakul bearing down on them. Getting them all out of this situation in one piece.

Domik shot a quick glance at CJ, who was sitting with her eyes squeezed shut, taking what looked to be forced deep breaths. He felt an almost uncontrollable urge to wrap her in his arms and tell her everything was going to be all right.

But he couldn't do that. For so many reasons.

The biggest being that he wasn't certain it would be all right. They were going into battle against a fierce enemy whose primary goal was to strip Earth of its current inhabitants and resources. Then the insectoid aliens would prepare the planet for their young, laying mass fields of eggs that the Xakul soldiers would protect with their lives. When the juvenile Xakul hatched, they would destroy everything in their path, consuming plants and animals indiscriminately.

They would destroy everything. Earth would be a husk, unlivable. Humanity would cease to exist.

Unless the Taurean and Human alliance could protect it from the Xakul threat.

Zac's voice was like a death knell for humanity. His next words sending a shiver down Domik's spine.

"It's just the Zataras now. We're on our own."

CHAPTER TWO

CJ

Blinking, CJ shook her head. How long had she been staring at the familiar blue and green planet on her station's view screen? She lifted a hand to adjust the comms headset and looked around the bridge of the small shuttle.

Zac's words rang in her head. *We're on our own.*

CJ swallowed, fighting to contain the bile that rose in her throat. It wasn't as if being on her own was anything new. Her father had left when she was a baby, then her mother had abandoned her with her grandmother when she was six years old to take a job on the other side of the country. She'd said she would be back in a few weeks. She never returned. And then, shortly after graduating from high school, her grandmother had died. The one person she had to rely on her whole life had gone.

Everybody leaves me.

CJ pushed the memories aside. That was the past. She was a different person now.

But are you really that different?

Yes. Her team—her friends—needed her to do her part. She could do this. She *had* to do this.

But you're a coward. You get scared and hide. How can they count on you?

She shoved the insidious thought aside.

That was one time. Once.

She sat up straight in her seat and blinked to clear her vision. The display in front of her showed the locations of the Taurean vessels nearest them. To contact an individual vessel, all CJ needed to do was touch the image of that vessel or state its call sign, and the comm channel would open.

When it was busy, the role of ship's communications officer was almost overwhelming. But when it was not busy... well, watching paint dry could sound appealing.

She lifted her wrist to check the comm. Only a minute had passed since the private message from the captain of the Zataras, Tomas Fa'Rell, had come through.

She turned in her seat and caught Domik's steady, dark gaze. One eyebrow lifted so slightly she would have missed it if she had blinked. On Domik, that was the equivalent of holding a megaphone in your hand and screaming for attention. She shivered, her heart thudding in her chest in a way that had nothing to do with the impending attack.

His eyes were dark brown, almost black, unlike most other Taureans who had lighter colored eyes, and his hair was similarly colored. He wore it long—when it was unbound; it fell down to his waist, though he usually wore it in a tight braid, the long end tucked in the back of his shirt to keep it out of the way. She had seen his hair loose only once, and the memory had never left her. He had been in the communal locker room at the gym they used on the Zataras. Domik had been sitting on a bench clad only in a towel, his head bent forward as he combed the tangles from his freshly washed hair. The towel he wore was barely held together at his hip, the fabric parting to show one thick thigh. That was the day that CJ had discovered that the bronze of his skin went all the way under his clothes. Domik did not have a single tan line. The white towel was so small that one small shift could send it tumbling toward the floor, and the sight had frozen her to the spot.

She had watched him for as long as she dared, mesmerized by the flex of his arms and shoulders as he pulled the comb through the long strands. The rhythm of his movements sending heat pooling to her groin. She must have made a noise as she watched him, because she would never forget the embarrassment of being caught staring. He'd looked up at her, and one side of his mouth had twitched, almost into a hint of a smile, and she'd been done for.

Almost eight feet of solid bronzed muscle, bulging biceps and thick thighs, and it had been that one brief twitch of his lips that had sent her tumbling into... what, exactly? She shied away from labeling how she felt. They were friends... weren't they?

And, right now, a friend was exactly what she needed. The familiarity—the solid comfort—of his expression soothed her frayed nerves, and she grinned.

"Everything all right, big guy?" She waggled her eyebrows as she spoke, eliciting a subtle snort of amusement. "I betcha that you'll break out in an actual smile any day now. It's only a matter of time until I wear you down."

His expression didn't change, but it wasn't unfriendly. He shook his head slightly, turning back to the weapons display.

So much for the crush she'd been nursing for months now. She couldn't figure out if he was interested in her as more than a friend. So they played chess, and she teased him to make him smile.

Domik did not smile.

But he would. For her. She'd make sure of it.

As long as they could get out of this mess.

CJ flicked a finger across the display in front of her, pulling up a screen that looked like an old school radar display, but in three dimensions. Their shuttle was in the center, and all the other Taurean ships were spread out around Earth. Very spread out.

She pulled up the visual from the cameras on the outside of the ship. It looked like something out of one of the science fiction films she'd loved as a child. There were hundreds of ships arranged in defensive formations, facing outwards from Earth. But there was far too much distance between the vessels. There were meant to be easily ten times the number of ships here. The Starship Zataras was in position, the hulking battleship an impressive sight, but it was the only battleship. The rest were cruisers and stealth ships, cargo vessels and pleasure craft.

Very few of the vessels were designed for combat, and CJ was relieved that theirs was one of them. And they had the best weapons specialist in the fleet in Domik.

She watched on the screen as T'arq eased their small battle shuttle quickly into place.

This was it. They were to stop the Xakul by any means necessary.

A beep in her earpiece notified her of an incoming transmission, a second beep designated a fleet-wide transmission.

"Incoming broadcast," she said and pressed a button, so they heard the voice over speakers in the bridge. Everyone stopped moving and silence filled the small space.

"This is the Zataras," the voice of that starship's Captain Tomas Fa'Rell filled the bridge. "Long-range sensors have identified multiple Xakul battleships. Estimated arrival in three minutes." There was a momentary pause, during which CJ could hear the rushing of blood in her ears. Tomas Fa'Rell's voice came over the speakers again. "Under no circumstances are they to reach the planet's surface. We know why they have come. They are here to destroy Earth. The Xakul want to strip the planet of its plentiful resources, leaving only devastation. You know we must prevent Earth's destruction. This is not a new fight, but this time, we have the enhanced cloak to shield us." Another pause followed, and then a loud battle cry filled the bridge. "For Taurus!"

CJ jumped in her seat as Zac and Domik both bellowed the cry in reply, "For Taurus!"

She shot a look at Krystal and Laila, who both grinned and, as one, the three women punched a fist into the air and yelled, "For Earth!"

CJ's eyes slid past the grinning face of Krystal, her brown curls bouncing as she turned to face T'arq, and instead focused on the sight before her.

Earth.

They were currently somewhere over the Pacific Ocean. If CJ's guess was right, this side of the planet was almost entirely blue water with clouds dotting the surface. The sight was awe-inspiring and the momentous nature of what they were about to attempt struck CJ like a brick.

Her arm dropped to her side, and she slumped in her seat, twisting to watch the slow rotation of the only planet she'd ever known as home. There suddenly wasn't enough air on the shuttle, and she struggled to breathe, her ribs tightening like a vice. She gasped, eyes filling with tears.

"Clodagh. I've got you." A deep rumble penetrated through the fog of her thoughts. A large, but surprisingly gentle, hand reached to turn her face. "It's going to be fine."

Dark eyes met hazel, and Domik's lips tilted in the tiniest move upwards. Barely a smile, but enough to bring one to her face. The tension released from her neck, and she rolled her shoulders.

"Nobody calls me that," she said quietly, before looking away.

He tilted his head toward her as if to say, "*I just did.*"

A beep in her earpiece had CJ's head whipping around to face the viewscreen in front of her. "This is the Zataras." Tomas' voice flowed over the speaker, the steady pace of his words flowing into the bridge. "The Xakul fleet has passed Jupiter. Expect enemy contact any moment." There was a pause. "The people of Earth are counting on us. Today we show what it means to stand united in the face of unrelenting evil."

A thick silence had descended on the bridge. CJ's heartbeat pounded in her ears, her breath sounding unnaturally loud.

"Today we join forces and—as our human allies would say—we blast these mother fuckers away!"

CJ couldn't help but laugh at the image of the very proper

starship captain shouting such profanity. But her good humor dissolved at his next words.

"I won't lie. These odds are not good. There will be casualties. But we have prevailed in far worse circumstances. And we will again today. Good luck."

"The Purist attack couldn't be a coincidence." CJ's ears pricked at Laila's muttered words to Zac, their heads bent together.

"You know how I feel about coincidences," he said in reply, lips pressed into a grim line.

CJ watched as Laila nodded slowly. "But what would they get out of it? It makes no sense."

CJ quietly agreed with her. The Taurean Purists were known for their fanatical belief in the sanctity of the Taurean race and were violently opposed to any 'blending' of Taureans with other races. They had not been quiet about their disapproval of the alliance between humans and Taureans, causing considerable political upheaval on Taurus, if the reports from the palace were to be believed. Karik Za'Rell, the Supreme Commander of Taurus, essentially the entire planet's leader, had even received death threats.

Domik's brother, Oren, had spent the last few weeks hunting down a small, but dangerous, splinter group. The only reason CJ even knew about that was because of a conversation she had overheard between Oren and Amelia. The doctor and the intelligence operative were not as discreet as they thought they were.

"Who knows what the Purists want? They're not known for their clarity of thought," Zac said, handing Laila a tablet. "Now, what do you think about this as a battle tactic?"

CJ turned away as the two began a detailed debate about the pros and cons of various formations.

From the corner of her eye she caught the view screen image flickering, automatically zooming in to showing an image from the Zataras' long-range sensors.

CJ's heart pounded as if it would burst from her chest. She rubbed her suddenly clammy palms on the legs of her flight suit as she leaned forward, transfixed.

The Xakul ships appeared, one by one, approaching ominously and with no attempt at deception. It was as if they knew the odds were in their favor.

Her brows drew together as she watched the dark shapes move closer.

"Cloak up!" Zac's voice rang loudly, jerking CJ back to the present.

"Cloak engaged, Commander," Krystal replied, staring intently at her tablet.

"Weapons free." Zac's voice was firm.

"Plasma weapons charged and ready." Domik's hands moved on his own console, his sure movements reassuring.

I can't do this. Not again. What if they need me and I fail them, like I did before?

Her chest tightened once more and her vision narrowed, the edges growing dark.

"Be calm, little sun." Domik's voice was soft as he captured her hand in one of his own and gave it a gentle squeeze. "I'm here. I won't let anything happen to you."

The tightness in CJ's chest eased at his words and she took a steadying, but shaky, breath.

"I'm not worried about me," she muttered, meeting his gaze. The panic she had felt dissolved, the tension in her body easing as her breathing calmed. Domik's fingers stroked gently over hers, and she focused on that small touch.

"No?"

"I just don't want to let anyone down," she said, adding under her breath, "Again."

His big fingers gave hers a gentle squeeze before letting go of her hand. "You won't."

CJ shook her head, fighting back tears. It was like Mars all over again, but this time she was out in the open with no place to hide. She felt her heart race once more, and she turned to look at Domik. He hadn't turned away, concerned eyes meeting hers. As long as she was with Domik, she would be OK. She smiled at him shakily, and he nodded in return before facing his station once more.

She turned back to her own console, watching as the Xakul ships gradually approached and then paused. They formed a wall of dark shapes hovering in a menacing way just beyond the range of the Taurean weapons.

"What are they doing?" Krystal asked.

"Testing us out." T'arq bit out. "We would have just disappeared on their sensors."

The cloaking technology refined by Krystal, with help from T'arq, had been rolled out across the fleet. Every ship currently in place around Earth would be invisible to the Xakul.

"Won't they suspect a trap?" CJ asked.

Zac nodded. "Yes, but that's not a bad thing. With our numbers so diminished, we need to do anything we can to delay their attack."

"Like shooting fish in a barrel," she muttered.

Zac's voice took on an urgent tone. "Incoming! Remember the drills we've practiced. The goal is to—"

As one the crew interrupted, saying, "Evade and destroy."

Zac nodded. "Let's do this."

The Xakul ships began moving closer, only to be fired upon as soon as they were in range of the Taurean guns.

The crew fell into their roles, T'arq swearing as he maneuvered them around Xakul and Taurean ships alike, avoiding both with a skill that left CJ in awe. Krystal began shouting navigation directions to him and tapping away frantically on a tablet, probably recording data on the cloak's performance. Zac and Laila worked together using the secondary guns to shoot at Xakul ships, as well as coordinating their movements with the nearby Taurean ships.

And Domik was in his element, brows drawn together as his hands moved over the controls of the weapons station, blasting Xakul ships one after the other.

CJ felt somewhat superfluous until a Xakul fighter shot the first Taurean ship down. "That's one of ours!" She watched, horrified, as the cloak disengaged and the ship blinked into existence on the viewscreen. A fireball engulfed the ship as it exploded, sending debris into nearby Taurean vessels. She looked on, horrified, as what could only be a body spun away from the wreckage, lifeless. The contrast of the peaceful beauty of Earth in the background was incongruous to the sudden terror that gripped her. She froze, hands hovering over her face in shock.

"CJ! Get on the comm! See if there are survivors!" Laila's order had CJ jerking in her seat, hands dropping to the controls.

"Yes, ma'am. Sorry. On it." She hailed the damaged ship, repeating her call until Domik's hand touched hers briefly.

"They're gone," he said simply.

CJ stared at him, her eyes huge in her pale face, as one thought shot through her with more certainty than anything she had ever felt.

We're going to die.

CHAPTER THREE

Domik

The battle raged around them as Domik readied the big guns and fired. A flash of green light lit the interior of the bridge, Domik blinking to clear his vision.

"That was close!" T'arq shouted, getting a grunt of acknowledgement from Zac.

Domik could operate all the ship's weapons from his station on the bridge, the craft's system feeding him a continuous stream of information on each of the big guns, as well as the smaller ones operated by Zac and Laila. These used plasma charges, which were shot at Xakul ships with devastating results. Domik checked the screen in front of him, his hands moving fast as he filtered through the streams of information, focusing on the mines that Laila had been dropping in the ship's wake. A Xakul ship blundered straight into one and immediately exploded, a fireball engulfing what remained of it.

Domik glanced to where CJ sat at the station next to his,

wasting precious seconds to check that she was all right. She was focusing on her own screen, deep in concentration, and Domik breathed a small sigh of relief. She had panicked earlier, and he had been worried about her. But she seemed to be OK. For the moment.

The Xakul had arrived as predicted, bringing numbers far greater than expected, and the Taurean fleet was doing everything they could to hold them back, but the sheer number of Xakul fighters meant that when one fell, another replaced it. The same could not be said for the Taurean fleet, and now gaps were appearing in the defenses.

Gaps that were not being filled.

With the Purist attack, Domik had doubts the backup would arrive in time. And now the speedy Xakul fighters had broken through the ranks and were terrorizing the slower Taurean battle craft.

The only advantage the Taureans had was their new cloaking technology, thanks to Krystal's modifications. And Domik had never been more thankful. T'arq and Krystal worked in unison; she charted a path through the increasingly complex battleground, while he flew the shuttle in ways that Domik couldn't understand. He was an absolute artist at the helm, but they were severely outnumbered, and it was only a matter of time before the Xakul got the better of them.

Their enemy was as intelligent as they were deadly, and they had figured out how to triangulate the shots fired to track down a Taurean shuttle. The Taureans had adapted, dodging as soon as they had fired, but they were slower to move and more than a few had been lost.

A shuttle next to them was hit, their cloak dropping as

soon as they lost power, and the two halves of the broken shift drifted apart.

Domik was thrown against his seat as T'arq dodged the debris, a second wayward shot from a Xakul fighter striking them and sending a shudder through their craft.

"Auto targeting is down!" Domik shouted. The blast must have damaged the controls for the big gun. He switched to manual targeting and pulled on the goggles that gave him a 3D view of the gun's position where it was mounted on the underside of the shuttle. He swung the barrel around and focused on the Xakul fighter that was approaching from beneath them and fired. The shuttle lurched as the big gun recoiled, and Domik reloaded.

CJ monitored the other ships, kept an ear on the comms, and alerted Domik to any potential targets for his large guns. She had saved them uncountable times already, her quick eyes and ears finding ships that were hidden to him behind debris.

Her voice reached him over the sounds of battle. "Domik! Xakul at—" The rest of what she said was lost as an explosion rocked the shuttle, sending them spinning.

Domik watched in horror as a Xakul ship bore down on them, the deadly plasma firing from its own guns barely missing them. He sighted on the enemy ship and fired; the shuttle lurching again and T'arq sending them into a rapid dive away and under their pursuer.

"The cloak isn't working!" Krystal's announcement had Domik swearing under his breath. They were as good as dead now.

His premonition seemingly came true a moment later as another blast sent them spinning, the lights of the bridge flickering before going out. An emergency klaxon sounded, the wail grating on Domik's nerves.

"Engines are down. We're not going anywhere." T'arq turned to Zac. "If we stay here, we're dead." The pilot's sentiment echoing Domik's own.

The commander nodded as smoke filled the bridge. "Agreed. To the escape pods. Now."

T'arq unstrapped from the pilot's seat and leaned down to scoop Krystal from hers before carrying her out of the bridge. Domik turned to CJ, whose face was white and her eyes huge as she looked at him in horror.

"Escape pods?" she whispered; her voice barely audible over the crunching of metal as the ship disintegrated around them.

"You've done the training. You'll be fine." He knew time was wasting. Every second they delayed could mean life or death, but she needed to be calm.

A hand on his shoulder had Domik turning to see Zac nodding toward the door. "Out. Now. Both of you."

CJ fumbled with the harness of her seat, her hands shaking as she tried to undo the buckle. Domik watched before brushing her hands gently aside and releasing her, pushing the harness from her shoulders and lifting her bodily from the seat.

"Hey! I can walk." She pushed against his chest, and he released her, relieved that she was showing her usual feisty nature.

Domik gestured for her to go first through the door, taking one last look around the bridge before following her into the smoke-filled hallway. As he walked, the shuttle shook, and he braced his hands on the hallway's walls as he staggered from side to side. An electrical fire broke out in the galley as they passed, sparks flying out from damaged appliances.

There were escape pods built into the top and base of the shuttle. Each held a single passenger with enough oxygen, water, and food to last a day or maybe two if a person opted to put themselves into stasis. There were eight escape pods on the shuttle, five below decks and three above, two more than the six who currently crewed the ship.

The access to both sets of pods was by ladders near the cargo bay to the rear of the ship. And it was here that they assembled.

Domik stood to one side, turning so he could monitor CJ, who was leaning against the wall, staring off into the distance. He moved next to her, and she wrapped her arms around herself as if seeking comfort.

The disquieting sound of the emergency siren was exacerbated as the overhead lighting flickered and dimmed, plunging them into darkness. A wail from Krystal was quickly stopped with a murmur from T'arq. As the emergency lights flickered on Domik saw that the short but curvaceous engineer had been enveloped in T'arq's arms, her head with its wild mass of bouncy brown curls cradled in one of his big hands as he pressed her close to his chest. T'arq's expression was serious, his lilac eyes concerned as they focused entirely on the woman cradled in his arms. His blond head bent toward hers as he whispered something, Krystal nodding and lifting her head to give the pilot a shaky smile.

The intimacy of the scene made Domik's chest squeeze, and he looked away as if watching was invading something private.

29

The emergency lights lit from the floor, with pulses directing away from their location and to the emergency escape pods. The lighting was a dull red glow, bathing the faces of his crewmates in ruby tones.

Domik hoped the eerie similarity to blood was not a sign of things to come.

Zac began handing out gas masks, which they all put on. "T'arq and Krystal, you take the lower pods. Domik and CJ, you take the upper pods. Laila and I will split between the two," he said, his gaze steady as he gestured toward the hatch that hid the ladder to the lower escape pods.

Krystal held up a hand, her expression hard to read behind the mask. "Uh, Zac? We might have a problem." She paused; her eyes huge as she looked up from the tablet. "It looks like we took a hit near the upper escape pods."

Fuck.

Domik ran a hand over his face. That was not good at all.

"Any idea how many pods are operational?" Zac asked, concern drawing his eyebrows together.

Krystal tapped at the tablet. "All the lower ones appear fine. I'm not sure about the upper ones. The data..." She lifted a shoulder in apology.

"OK. Everyone to the lower pods. I'll take an upper one," Zac said with a decisive nod, turning to grasp the ladder to the upper level.

Laila put her hand on his arm, stilling him. Apart from her height, Laila looked very much like her sister. Both had brown, almost amber, colored eyes, and brown, curly hair. But where Krystal's hair was loose in a mass of bouncy curls, Laila pulled hers back in a no-nonsense military-style bun. And both women were looking at their men—their Taurean warriors—with serious expressions. "I'll come with you," Laila said.

Zac whipped around to look at her. "No. You won't." Their eyes locked, and both scowled intensely, Zac's scarred face taking on a sinister appearance, but that didn't bother Laila one bit.

Domik looked around the group. Laila and Zac needed each other. They had only recently married and the thought of only one of them not making it out alive... well, Domik couldn't live with himself if he hadn't tried his hardest to prevent that. Then there were T'arq and Krystal, whose fledgling relationship had changed T'arq in ways that Domik would never have believed possible. The former playboy pilot was still confident, but he had lost the cocky edge. It was like he no longer felt the need to prove himself. And Krystal? She had hated flying before she met T'arq and now she was his flight engineer, the two making an unparalleled team. No, they needed to make it off this shuttle. Together.

And then there was CJ. He watched as she leaned against the wall, her head bowed and her arms wrapped around herself as she shook. Was she more injured than she had let on?

He turned toward her, resting a hand on her shoulder. She looked up at him, blinking to clear her glazed eyes. She was terrified; her breathing was fast and her eyes wild.

Zac and Laila were still arguing, but stopped as Domik cleared his throat and spoke. "I'll go."

Laila protested, but Domik cut her off.

"You all have someone. I have nobody. I'll go."

CJ gasped at his statement, but he refused to look at her, instead turning to face Zac.

"Are you sure about this?" Zac asked.

"I am." Domik's certainty that this was the right move only increased as he spoke.

"For Taurus," Zac said grimly. Domik didn't reply, just clasped his commander's outstretched arm in a warrior's greeting, grunting in surprise as Zac pulled him close to touch foreheads in the way of close friends.

Domik watched as Zac bent to lift the hatch to the lower level escape pods, a plume of smoke rising as he did so. Adjusting his mask, he descended into the gloom. Domik stood at the base of the ladder to the upper escape pods and watched as, one by one, they disappeared into the hatch below.

When it was CJ's turn, she looked up at him and hesitated. "Domik?" She asked, her face behind the mask pale and drawn.

"You can do this. I'll see you back on the Zataras." He nodded, hoping to encourage her, and she looked down into the smoky depths, steeled her shoulders, and climbed down the ladder. Domik watched as she disappeared into the smoke.

T'arq was the last one down, lifting a hand in farewell to Domik and quickly descending toward the escape pods.

That was that then. He was alone. Now to get out of here.

Domik turned his back on the lower hatch and climbed toward the upper pods.

CHAPTER FOUR

CJ

With every step she took down the ladder, CJ's heart sank further and further. It just didn't feel right to leave someone behind. Who was she kidding? It didn't feel right leaving Domik behind. Her stomach rolled at the thought of him being stranded on the damaged shuttle. What if the upper pods were damaged, and they left him behind? How could she ever live with herself?

I should have stayed with him!

Her foot slipped on the rung, her hands burning as they slid down the metal of the ladder before she stopped with a jerk as her feet hit the next rung. A jolt of pain shot through her legs, and she gasped hot air, the mask she wore thankfully keeping her from breathing in smoke.

He said he would meet you on the Zataras. He keeps his promises.

She clung to the ladder, her heart racing as she tried to

33

MELODY BECKETT

calm her breathing. She could do this. Everything would be OK when she got to the escape pod.

The smoke was thick down here, and she struggled to see through the haze. She made her way down the last few rungs before her feet reached the sturdy metal grid of the floor.

Through the crisscrossed grid, she could see the lower part of the ship where the engines were housed. Sparks flew and smoke choked the air, and she quickly dropped to her knees to escape the worst of it.

She whipped around, looking for anyone in the gloom, and spotted a shape as the smoke shifted around her. The smoke cleared to show T'arq gesturing at her to hurry.

CJ crawled toward him, the torn skin of her hands smarting on the hot metal of the floor. She gritted her teeth and tried to breathe shallowly behind her mask, but couldn't prevent a gasp of pain when a sharp edge dug into her palm.

Her heartbeat pounded in her ears, the sound of the ship tearing apart and the klaxon wailing making her head pound. Slowly, one hand in front of the other, she made her way to the escape pods.

I can do this. I can do this.

She ran the thought like a mantra through her head, trying not to think about the small escape pod that was her only hope of getting off the shuttle alive. They were like metal coffins, an image that CJ had fought to clear from her mind the first time she had seen them, but it persisted. In training, they had practiced using the pods to escape, but training and an actual emergency were very different.

She should know.

This is nothing like that.

She fought back the intrusive thoughts, pushing them

34

aside and focusing on putting one foot—or one hand—in front of the other and slowly making it closer to safety.

A loud bang and a shudder had CJ flinching and sliding across the floor as the ship titled ominously. A scream rent the air, and a sudden gap in the smoke gave CJ a view of a prone form, blood spilling in a pool beneath them.

"No!" she shouted, staggering to her feet and taking an unsteady step toward the body. She doubled over as a cough wracked her chest. Eyes streaming from the smoke, she could barely make out what was happening.

This couldn't be happening. Not again. Never again.

A loud screech had her frozen, eyes wide in fright, gasping for air that wasn't there.

That noise. No, it couldn't be...?

There was another screech, followed by a crash. As the shuttle shook, CJ fell to her knees once more and fought for breath.

There are no Xakul here. It's just the shuttle breaking apart.

CJ laughed, knowing she was bordering on hysterical. To her, the idea of a space shuttle breaking up was better than there being Xakul soldiers on the ship. And then the smoke cleared a little, and she rubbed at her eyes. The body was... sitting up?

The tension in CJ's chest eased as she watched Zac bend to say something to Laila. CJ crawled forward, belatedly remembering that it was she, as the medic, who should take care of any injured.

"Laila? Are you OK?" she asked as she approached, pushing back her fright and focusing on the dazed woman in front of her. Her training kicking in, CJ ran through the series of checks to see how badly her friend was hurt.

"Yeah, I think so. I must have hit my head," the older woman said, rubbing her temple. She smiled wryly and CJ chuckled, relieved that she was simply dazed and not seriously hurt.

"Can you get her into the escape pod?" CJ asked, turning to Zac.

"Yes." He scooped her up into his arms and slid her gently into the waiting pod. It was shaped like an egg, if a little stretched out to accommodate the taller stature of the Taurean warriors. There was a seat that, when she had first seen an escape pod, had reminded CJ of a dentist's chair, as well as a series of controls built into the walls of the pod. The door was like a hatch, but one that slid into a recess in the pod itself, and in the door was a small window. It was through the opening of the pod that Laila now peered at Zac.

"You'll be there? When we make it back to the Zataras?" Laila asked, clinging to Zac's hand.

He smiled and brushed her hair back from her face. "I promise."

CJ took a step back, giving the couple some space, and turned to find Krystal already settling into her pod. Krystal gripped T'arq hand tightly, reluctantly letting go to shut the door, the pod sealing with a hiss as it pressurized. The second set of doors to the shuttle itself closed, a small window the only way to see the pod. Krystal waved from inside as the light on the outside flickered from green to red, and the pod disengaged, leaving an empty cavity in the shuttle's side. CJ watched as Krystal's pod quickly moved away and toward the Starship Zataras in the distance, before the pod's cloak engaged and it disappeared. T'arq quickly got into his own pod, and within seconds had ejected from the shuttle and was following Krystal back to the Zataras.

CJ turned, stumbling along the row of pods toward one of two empty ones. Was Domik able to get away? She couldn't imagine a world where Domik wasn't able to overcome anything thrown at him. He faced down all threats with a solid dependability that made concrete look like jelly. Thinking of Domik calmed CJ's rapidly beating heart.

She reached an empty pod and hit the button to open the hatch, before turning to see Zac settle Laila into her pod, pressing a series of buttons on the outside before closing the doors to the shuttle and ejecting it to follow in T'arq and Krystal's wake.

Zac gestured for CJ to climb into her pod. "Get into your pod. I won't leave until you do."

CJ peered into the pod, the small coffin-like space making her skin crawl.

Krystal did it, and she used to be terrified of flying. You can do this. It's not like the freezer at all.

The dull silver of the metal was warm against her skin as she reached a hand out to open the doors. The cooler air in the pod rushed out, sending goosebumps over her skin.

You have to do this. It's the only way.

The seat was comfortable; she noted with surprise, and she settled into it, pulling the harness over her shoulders and up from between her legs to connect in the middle.

Zac hit the button on the outside of her pod and the doors slid shut. He gave her a small smile before turning and leaving; the smoke swirling behind him was a stark reminder of how urgent this situation was.

Just hit the button, and then you're safe.

She took a deep breath and hit the button that would eject the pod from the ship.

Nothing happened.

What the fuck?

She hit the button again.

Nothing.

Mashing the button for all she was worth, she banged again and again.

Nothing.

This could not be happening.

She threw her head back against the cushion of the seat, closing her eyes and taking deep breaths.

I have to get out of here. Now.

CJ pushed the button to open the doors to the shuttle and, with a wave of relief, they opened, sending a plume of smoke into the pod.

She coughed, pulling the mask over her face once more, and clambered out of the pod. Had Zac left? He could help her, surely? She looked down the row of pods, and with a sinking feeling, counted.

Five pods. Four ejected. He'd gone. And the last one was malfunctioning.

Fuck. Fuck. Fuck.

But there were eight on the ship. She just had to get to the other ones. The ones where Domik had gone. The ones that had likely been damaged by fire from a Xakul ship.

Don't think about that.

Dropping to her knees, the metal grid biting through the fabric of her flight suit and into the skin of her legs, she mashed the button on her wrist comm.

"Domik? Domik? Are you still here?" Her voice was hoarse from the smoke, and she began coughing.

No reply.

Was she all alone on this shuttle?

Why am I not surprised?

She slumped forward onto her hands, gripping the metal grid as an uncontrollable coughing fit wracked her chest. Eyes streaming, CJ fell to her side, curling into a ball and hugging her knees to her chest.

So this is how I die.

Another blast shook the shuttle, the floor tilting underneath her. She rolled across the floor, slamming into the wall with enough force that she cried out. A sharp pain shot through her side as she took a breath. She clutched her rib cage, gasping acrid, smoky air.

A rib. I must have cracked a rib.

She forced herself to her knees, clutching her side with one hand and the wall with the other. There were eight escape pods. There was still a chance she could escape. Gritting her teeth, she braced herself against the wall. The floor of the shuttle tilted to one side in a way that suggested the artificial gravity was on its way out.

Slowly, she made her way back to the ladder that led up to the main floor of the shuttle, keeping low out of the billowing smoke. One shuffling step on her knees after another. Something sparked below her, sending a wave of heat from her feet, and still she pushed forward, teeth gritted against the pain of her smarting hands and the rib that pulsed pain through her chest with every breath.

Just as she spied the ladder through the haze of smoke, the emergency lighting went out, plunging her into darkness.

Her breath sounded unnaturally loud as she blinked, trying desperately to see in the gloom.

Don't panic. The ladder is just ahead. You saw it.

She pressed forward, fumbling in the dark with an outstretched hand until she reached the ladder, hissing as the torn skin of her palm contacted with the metal. She ground her teeth against the pain, gripping the rungs as she pulled herself upright.

A flood of relief washed over her when she took the first rung and moved upwards toward the main floor of the shuttle.

"Thank fuck for that," she muttered, as she made her way, one slow rung after another to the hatch above.

She pushed against the hatch and, thankfully, it lifted easily, and she pulled herself up and onto the main floor. Legs still in the open hatchway, she flopped down on her back, breathing as heavily as her ribs would allow.

The emergency lighting on this level was still working, but flickering ominously. She would have to hurry.

She rolled to one side and pushed herself up onto her knees and then to her feet, each step like walking through mud. In a distant part of her brain, she knew it was from a lack of oxygen. One foot in front of the other. She made it the few steps toward the second ladder that led up to the upper level where the remaining escape pods were.

Placing one foot on the bottom rung, she climbed, the smoke quickly becoming so thick she couldn't see her hands. She coughed, almost losing her grip on the ladder.

Clinging desperately with both hands, she frantically felt around for the latch that would release the hatch into the upper level.

Where was it?

She hadn't made it this far to fail now. She banged against the hatch, knowing it was useless. Nobody was there. They'd all left. And now she would die.

She thumbed the comm on her wrist one last time. "Domik? Anyone? Help me!"

CHAPTER FIVE

Domik

The shuttle shook for what felt like the thousandth time since Domik had climbed up into the upper level. It had felt wrong leaving CJ down there, but he knew she would be safe. Zac wouldn't leave until he knew she was safely in an escape pod.

Domik shut the hatch to the lower level, blocking off the smoke that was rapidly billowing in. The fumes made his eyes water and his throat felt raw from coughing. He blinked rapidly and scanned the escape pods.

He wasn't able to stand upright in this space. In fact, he couldn't stand at all. It was more a crawl space, designed for accessing some exterior electrics and weaponry. It was because of the plasma guns mounted on the top of the vessel that Domik was very familiar with this part of the shuttle.

He slid forward on his hands and knees toward the escape pods. The floor was made of panels of lightweight metal that clicked together for easy access if one needed to be pulled up. The walls were of the same material, a dull matte gray color that most Taurean military vessels were. Each of the escape pods was barely large enough to fit a Taurean of Domik's size. He'd been in one before. All warriors were required to train in their use, and it had been a tight fit for most, but especially for Domik, who was larger than the average Taurean man. It certainly was not a comfortable trip that he would be taking.

But it will save your life. Such as it is.

He grunted at the thought. His life was a series of days filled with superficial interactions, or it had been. Shaking his head to clear the thoughts of the blond medic, Domik slid closer to the nearest escape pod.

A blinking red light lit the panel. Domik's lips pressed together in a grim line as he looked through the small window. The pod had taken the brunt of a Xakul blast that had ripped a large hole in its side. It was a miracle that the shuttle itself hadn't been damaged.

The second pod was in the same state, damaged from what looked to Domik like some kind of plasma spray.

One more to go.

His heart thumped rapidly in his chest as he approached the final pod. If this one was damaged too... well, he didn't want to think about that.

A green light lit up the display.

Domik released a long, shaky breath, eyes closed in relief.

He hit the button on the door to open the pod.

Nothing happened.

Fuck.

That wasn't unexpected, considering how much damage the ship had taken. He looked through the window and into the pod. It didn't look like there was any visible damage. The pod looked... like an escape pod.

With such a genius intellect, is it any surprise you are single?

Domik sighed. There was nothing for it but to get out the tools.

There wasn't enough room to turn around in the small space, so he had to roll onto his back and fiddle with the pocket on his combat pants where he had kept a multi-tool. The thing had been useful on more than one occasion, and he hoped today would be no exception.

Wriggling back into place, he prized open the access panel next to the pod door, pulling out a mess of singed cables, damaged beyond repair.

With a sigh, he dropped the mess and dragged a hand over his head, smoothing the stray strands that had escaped the braids that held the dark mass back during battle.

He closed his eyes and lay still for a second, running through his options.

A faint noise made his ears prick up, barely audible over the creaking of the ship's hull and the klaxons that were still wailing away in the background.

Bang. Bang. Bang.

There it was again. A consistent banging that had to be coming from someone. Domik checked his comm. Enough time had passed that everyone should have left on the escape pods. There should be nobody left.

Unless there was a problem with the pods.

Domik wriggled across the floor to the hatch, levering it open with some difficulty. A wave of heat and smoke greeted him, and he threw an arm up to shield his face, holding his breath against the rush of acrid air.

A small hand reached up and grasped his own where it was curled around the edge of the hatch.

"Domik?" CJ's voice was weak. "I thought I was alone. I thought everyone had gone."

Reaching down, he slid his hands under her arms and lifted her easily through the hatch to sit on the edge. "Quick, we need to shut the hatch." He helped her lift her legs clear and banged the hatch shut, pushing the locking latch into place.

Her eyes were red and watery in a face streaked with dirt and black smudges. Her blond hair was plastered to her head with sweat, her flight suit torn at the knees and elbows.

It had only been minutes since he'd last seen her, but she looked like she'd weathered years. He pulled her into his arms and clasped her against his chest as he smoothed a hand over her hair.

She was alive.

He pulled back slightly to look at her. "What happened?" He grasped her by the shoulders, unable to prevent himself from touching her. He needed to make sure she was real. That she was alive.

"The pod... it wouldn't go."

Domik pressed his lips together. She must have been terrified.

"So I came up here..." she trailed off, biting her lip as her eyes filled with tears. "Are we going to die, Dom?"

He couldn't answer her. There was only one pod left. If he could get the door open. And there were two of them.

The decision was simple.

Domik let her go and made his way back to the pod. The

panel with the dangling wires greeted him as if to mock his earlier attempts at escape.

There was only one thing for it.

Why be this big if it isn't of any use?

With grim determination, he jammed the doors open with his multi-tool, just enough to get his fingers into the gap. Then, muscles straining, he pulled them apart with all his might.

"Domik! What are you doing?" CJ cried, unable to see past him in the small space.

"Opening.... the... doors!" He grunted with exertion, teeth gritted, arms bulging as he pulled the doors open. With one final yell of exertion, they pulled apart, and by some miracle, stayed open.

Domik flopped to the floor, exhausted. A small hand landed on his forehead, smoothing back his hair, concerned hazel eyes peering down into his.

"How many pods are working, Dom?" she asked, one eyebrow lifted as if she knew the answer already but needed him to confirm it.

He turned his head to one side, refusing to answer. Her fingers were like steel as she turned his chin, so he was looking at her.

"Dom?" She lifted the other eyebrow. He knew that expression. His chest clenched as he tilted his head toward the pod he had just opened. She glanced at where he showed, glancing back at him. "Just one?"

He nodded, closing his eyes and letting his head flop back against the metal grille of the floor.

"Fuck." She flopped back onto the floor next to him.

He grunted in agreement.

The shuttle shook once more, and he grabbed the woman who plagued his every waking, and often sleeping, thought, pulling her to his side as if to protect her from anything that would hurt her.

"You'll have to take it," she said, half sitting up.

He rocked bolt upright, hitting his head on the low ceiling. He huffed in annoyance, rubbing his head with one hand while he glared at her. "No. I'll stay."

The infuriating woman shook her head. "No. You're needed more, Dom. You take the pod."

Domik scowled at her. "I have nobody. You go."

"And I have someone?" She scoffed. "You have a brother. A family who I'm sure loves you. I don't have a family. I don't have anyone. Go." She gave him a gentle push as if she could move his giant form into the pod.

"You have me." His confession surprised them both, and they stared at each other for a long moment before she shook her head slowly. Her eyebrows drew down and, if he could see her mouth behind the mask, he was certain she would purse her lips at him in frustration.

"I'll put on a spacesuit and float around until someone picks me up."

The thought made Domik's stomach churn. "No. You'd be ripped apart. I won't allow it."

CJ's eyebrows shot up so fast they almost disappeared into her hair. "You won't allow it?"

Danger. Danger.

And it wasn't from the shuttle that was about to explode all around them. Domik rubbed his temples. He never used his sheer size against a woman, but he had no choice. He turned and pressed the button on the exterior of the pod itself, holding his breath in anticipation as the lights flicked green and the doors opened.

He closed his eyes, sighing in relief before grabbing CJ bodily by the arms and, as gently as he could, lifting her into the escape pod. She, predictably, kicked and flailed her arms and legs, grabbing the edge of the door as he pushed her inside.

He was just about to press the button to shut the door to the pod itself when she grabbed his arms and half pulled herself out of the pod. As much as he could tell from under the filth coating her face, the blood had run from her face and she was panting, eyes glazed.

"It's going to be all right. Just get in the pod, Clodagh."

His use of her full name had her eyes snapping to his, her hands tightening where they gripped his arms. "What did you call me?"

And this time, his lips tilted just a little. "Your name." He knew that would get her. He'd only found out by accident, but in his own mind that's what he called her. It suited her, and he liked the way her name felt on his tongue.

"You're the only one who calls me that, you know." She tilted her head to one side, as if trying to understand some complex mathematical problem.

Another blast shook the shuttle, and she gasped, the moment broken. The blasts were coming more frequently now. They had minutes, if they were lucky, but probably more like seconds, until the ship was torn completely apart.

"Go." His tone was urgent. He had to get her off this shuttle.

"No. Not without you." The stiff way she held herself, telling him she would not give in.

Stubborn woman.

He was big enough that he could overpower her, but the thought was abhorrent. "Listen. We both won't fit. And there's not enough oxygen for two. Get in or we'll both die!" Domik felt an unaccustomed anxiety flood him at the thought of her not making it to safety.

"If we pull something out, I bet we could both fit in here." She gestured behind her with one hand toward the miniscule pod.

He looked past her shoulder, assessing the space.

Why didn't I think of that?

He was not a small Taurean, and although she was slim, she was tall. At least for a human. When they stood, she reached the middle of his chest, so in the pod... well, she would have to sit on his lap.

The thought had him shifting uncomfortably.

Not the time and definitely not the place.

But he knew what these pods were like. There was no room to move when he got in there himself. It would be very uncomfortable. But it might just work.

Domik jerked his head, gesturing for her to climb back out. CJ quickly clambered from the pod. An ominous creaking noise sounded from above their heads, both of them freezing to stare at the ceiling.

If they were going to do this, they needed to do it fast. And they would need supplies. "Go through the hatches and see what you can find that can be used as padding." Domik pointed toward a row of locker style hatches opposite the pods.

CJ nodded and began opening and closing doors as she pulled all manner of things out, throwing things into a pile and clutching others to her chest. Domik turned to the pod and, with a sigh, yanked the seat free from its bolts, pulling it into the shuttle. Without the seat, it really looked like a metal can, like he'd seen in some of the Earth movies he had watched. Ones that he'd overheard CJ talking about.

What did the humans say, something about small fish crammed in a can?

"Will a couple of blankets do?" CJ asked, holding out a simple Taurean military issue blanket. It was thin, but it would be better than nothing.

"Yes. Let's go." Domik lay the blanket down in the pod where the seat had been, and climbed in. He shifted around, trying to make as much space for CJ as possible.

"Ready?" she asked, biting her lip as she watched him.

He nodded, holding out his hand for hers. "Come," he said.

She bit back a choked laugh. "Under different circumstances." She slid her fingers into his own, his larger hand swallowing hers.

"Do you always joke when you are scared?" Domik asked, grasping her fingers and tugging her gently.

She gasped as she slid into the pod, landing on his chest, her face so close to his he could count her eyelashes. Her slight weight was not unpleasant, even feeling right in a way nothing else ever had. He lifted a hand to rest in the middle of her back, holding her snugly against him.

"No," she breathed. "Not usually."

She was so close that he could see flecks of green and gold in her eyes, the combination deeply beautiful. Domik broke away with difficulty, using his free hand to close the pod doors. A hiss as the door snapped shut, and the pod pressurized. They were enclosed. Together. Alone.

CJ wriggled on top of him, her breath coming in short pants.

Domik's hand smoothed up and down her back in slow strokes. He made low, soothing noises in his throat and she stilled, her head resting against his chest as she took a slow breath.

"Domik?" Her voice was small.

"Hmm?"

"Thank you for not leaving me."

He stilled. Leave her? Never. Not while he still had breath in his lungs. Not while his heart still beat. All the words he had held back rushed forward in a flood, and he pressed his lips tight to keep them back.

A loud boom, and a flash of light blinded him and, instinctually, he slapped his hand against the button to eject the pod from the ship.

As the pod disengaged, Domik stared through the window in the pod's doors as the shuttle filled with flames. Doing some quick calculations in his head, he realized they had mere seconds to be clear of the vessel before it was engulfed. The vacuum of space would only do so much. They had to be clear.

A helpless feeling washed over him, his stomach dropping like a stone.

Were they too late?

CHAPTER SIX

CJ

She stared in horror as the flames licked at the doors of the pod. She felt her heart race faster and faster, her vision narrowing as she panted for air that just didn't seem to be there.

I'm going to die. I'm going to burn alive or suffocate in space. Or both. At the same time.

She gasped, dragging air into her lungs.

The pod disengaged from the shuttle with a jerk, and then they were moving away, but not fast enough for CJ's liking.

The walls of the pod pressed in on her, the space taken up by their bodies leaving no room to move. It was warm, and she struggled, thrashing around as she fought to get free. Her breathing became ragged as she lost control and began gasping for air.

Ripping the mask she still wore off, she turned her face

away from Domik's chest and sucked in delicious mouthfuls of cool, clean air.

"Oh god! Oh god! We're going to die!" she cried; eyes wild as she stared up at him.

"Hush," Domik said, his deep voice soothing and calm, breaking through her terror. "I have you. I won't let anything happen to you."

And she believed him. Her thrashing stilled, and she sagged in his arms. CJ forced herself to keep looking up at him, calming her breathing.

He wriggled an arm up to remove his face mask, tossing it down near their feet. A lighter triangle of bronze skin around his mouth and nose contrasted with the dark smudges around his eyes. Such dark eyes, the color of obsidian. Dark and dangerous. Deep and soulful. Strands of his hair floated around his head that had come loose from the thick braid that ran down the back of his head. The sides shaved to the skin, showing dark stubble, gave him a dangerous appearance, like a Nordic warrior of old.

"You will not die. Not today." He stated, simply.

"No?"

He shook his head, smoothing his hand down her back and hummed in a low tone. Was he... singing to her?

A shudder shook the pod, and he lifted his hand to cradle her head against his chest as if to protect her

"What was that?" She squeezed her eyes shut, hands clenched tightly into fists against his chest, grabbing his flight suit.

"Explosion from the shuttle. Look," he said, tilting his head toward the small window in the pod's door.

CJ gasped at the sight spread out in front of them, like a

space battle from a science fiction movie. The great expanse of Earth was spread out below. Darkness was descending, and millions of lights marking human cities, towns and industry twinkled beneath them. Against that backdrop, Xakul fighters shot every which way, zooming into and out of sight as quickly as CJ could blink. Shots of plasma appeared to take them down, looking like the fire appeared from nowhere, but really came from a cloaked Taurean ship.

As she watched, three Xakul ships fired in unison, apparently at nothing, and a Taurean ship lurched into being, the cloak damaged in the attack. CJ buried her head into Domik's chest as she watched the Taurean vessel break up on impact, a series of explosions firing bright orange and winking out as quickly as they had started.

Nearest to them, the now almost unrecognizable mass of their shuttle broke apart, a small fireball winking out quickly and debris flying away from the craft. A Xakul ship appeared, flying straight at their pod, eliciting a strangled scream from CJ as she screwed her eyes shut and braced for a blast from the enemy guns that never came.

"We're cloaked. They can't see us," Domik soothed, his hand running down her back once more.

Keep it together. You can't show how weak you are.

"Oh, of course." She gave a forced chuckle that sounded fake to her own ears. She was suddenly aware of just how much of Domik she could feel. He was a solid wall of muscle. Very warm muscle. Her booted feet were nestled between his legs, which were splayed open as far as the small pod would allow. Her knees were tucked in between his thighs, which brought the apex of her legs right in line with the significant bulge of his cock.

Don't think about his dick.

The problem was, when you tried not to think about something, the opposite happened. CJ's thoughts were flooded with images of Domik half-naked in change rooms after physical training, water running down his broad chest and over abs that disappeared into tiny running shorts.

What was it with Taureans and tiny running shorts?

He had the thickest thighs she had ever seen on a man. Male. Alien. Whatever. They were bigger than both of hers put together, and his ass?

CJ wriggled, trying to put some distance between her and Domik, but only making the situation worse as the thickness that nestled against her sex seemed to swell against her. The only sign that her movement had impacted Domik was a slight stiffening of his arms around her. And the slight stiffening of his—

Don't think about it!

"So, what's next?" CJ asked, turning her head to watch as the wrecked shuttle grew smaller, and releasing the handfuls of Domik's flight suit she had gripped into tight fists.

Domik's hand stilled on her back. "The pods are programmed to return to the Zataras."

CJ nodded. She remembered that from the training. The pods were programmed to return to whichever battleship the shuttle was attached to. Unless, of course, the programming was overridden, which could be done from inside the pod. Or unless they were damaged.

The escape pods were designed for one person, with enough oxygen to survive for a day or two at most. There was a medi-wand and a data tablet in each pod, as well as a pack of emergency rations that, if someone had been checking the pods regularly, should still be edible.

But how long could the two of them survive in a pod designed for one?

And would they even make it back to the Zataras? Given how chaotic the fighting was, it was debatable if they would even make it back through the mass of space junk that now littered the expanse between them and the big battleship.

Where was that tablet? If she could get to it, she could check their oxygen levels and work out how long they had.

There was a small hatch in the wall opposite the passenger's seat, so that would mean it was behind her. CJ wriggled around, trying to get her hand to find the latch, but they were so cramped she could not do so.

"Stop." Domik's voice was pained.

She ignored the command, twisting around to get her hands on the panel. His arm dragged her against him, and with sudden clarity, she realized why he'd asked her to stop. She was pressed from head to toe up against Domik. His muscular torso was warm against her, and a very solid and thick bar was pressed against the seam of her pants.

Oh.

She stilled, flushing and looking up at him through sooty eyelashes. He wasn't looking at her, instead staring at something above her head with an intensity that would have melted her panties off.

"Sorry," she said quietly. "I was just trying to get the tablet."

Domik grunted, moving his hand behind her back. A few seconds later, he offered the tablet to her, which she took with a smile of thanks.

She flicked it on and scrolled through to check the stats of the pod.

"So, we have twelve hours of oxygen remaining... and the cloak is still intact, as you thought." She sighed in relief, thankful that their primary protection was still in place.

Domik's chest rumbled underneath her. "What about the autopilot?"

CJ's brows furrowed as she flicked through to the relevant screen. "Working fine." She smiled up at him. "We should be fine—"

A blast cut off her words and she let out a shriek of fright, clutching at Domik and dropping the tablet to clatter against the side of the pod, then float somewhere around their shoulders.

Domik made a grab for the tablet and handed it back to her. "We will survive this." His words were calming to her, and she nodded.

"I just..."

"Shhh, it's OK." He brushed his hand over the back of her head, crooning to her in his deep baritone rumbling through her as he smoothed her hair back.

She relaxed against his chest, somehow soothed by this giant of a warrior who could crush her in one hand, should he wish. Something in her heart shifted, and she felt the walls she had built up around herself crack—just a little.

"I locked myself in a freezer, you know." She surprised herself by speaking the words she had never said before. To anyone. "On Mars. During the Xakul attack."

"I know."

"You know?" She looked up in surprise. "How?" He just raised an eyebrow slightly. She huffed out a breath. "I suppose word gets around, doesn't it?" She shook her head. "I hate small spaces," she whispered.

Domik said nothing, just letting her speak and rubbing a hand up and down her back, the motion calming. She relaxed a little, and the words tumbled out. About how she had survived the Mars attack by hiding in a freezer in the morgue and staying quiet. How she had heard the screams as people were slaughtered by the Xakul soldiers and had done nothing.

"I should have done something. Every time I think about what happened, I tell myself I should have fought, but I was so scared." She gulped lungfuls of air as she rapidly blinked, trying to ease the stinging of her eyes.

Domik lifted his hand and captured one of her tears, rubbing it between his thumb and forefinger. His gaze was intent as he turned to her. "You would have been slaughtered. Just like the others. I am glad you weren't."

Her mouth fell open as she stared up at him. Then, remembering herself, she cleared her throat. "Do you think everyone made it back to the Zataras?"

Domik checked his wrist comm. "They've had enough time." He took the tablet from her listless fingers and tapped at the screen. "That's odd." His eyebrows drew together.

"What's wrong?"

"The tablet has—" Domik stopped and dropped the tablet, looking out the pod's window and swearing under his breath.

"What?" CJ asked, before looking at where he was staring.

Spread before them was a sight like none she had ever seen. Ships, Xakul and Taurean alike, had stopped firing. And the Taurean ships were now visible, their cloaks no longer hiding them from view.

As CJ watched, a Xakul ship spun listlessly, colliding with a Taurean ship and sending it spinning away, uncontrolled.

"Domik? What's going on?" She breathed.

"I think the Xakul have released an EMP," he said, gazing out the window, transfixed.

"A what?" CJ had never heard of such a thing, but whatever it was, it must be something powerful enough to render all the ships inert. But why would the Xakul do such a thing to their own ships as well as the Taureans? It made no sense.

"I've heard of this happening, but..." he trailed off.

CJ's brows drew together in frustration. "Domik, what's an EMP?"

He blinked, focusing on her again. "It stands for electromagnetic pulse." She must have still looked confused as he continued. "Have you heard of solar storms?"

She nodded.

"An EMP has a similar effect. It wipes out all electronic equipment within its range, rendering it unusable."

"Oh." CJ paused. "So all the ships..."

"Are dead."

"For how long?"

Domik shrugged. "It depends on how powerful the EMP was, but considering that—" He pointed to the planet below, where night was soon to fall. CJ blinked as she realized why it looked so strange. There were only a handful of lights scattered across the vast area that would normally be lit up like a Christmas tree.

"Shit." She breathed.

"Exactly."

"What do we do?"

Domik took a deep breath, as if steeling himself to deliver news that she wouldn't like.

"Just tell me, Domik." She scowled, not enjoying being kept in the dark. Literally, as it would seem.

"We can try to get to the Zataras," he said, gesturing back through the mass of ships spread out in front of them.

CJ watched as two Xakul vessels crashed together, wincing as they crushed a Taurean ship in between them. She didn't like their chances of making their way back through that. If they could get the little manual thrusters on the pod working.

"Is there an alternative?" she asked hopefully.

"Yes," he said, his voice a deep pit of grim.

"Are you going to tell me what it is?" She asked, a hint of sarcasm coloring her words.

He jerked his head toward the planet below. "We try our luck down there."

"But that's suicide!" She gasped.

"We don't have the luxury of waiting for someone to come and get us. If we weren't in the middle of an active battlefield sure, that would be an option. But, right now?" He shook his head. "I don't like our chances."

CJ shook her head in denial. "No, we have to stay."

"We're too exposed to take that risk, CJ." His voice was irritatingly calm, while her guts were tied up in knots. Domik blinked, expression unreadable. "If we stay, we die. What's it to be?"

CHAPTER SEVEN

Domik

He hated putting her in this position, but she needed to feel like the decision was hers. It was obvious to Domik that she was struggling with being in the pod with him. He knew it wasn't ideal. She would probably want to be stuck with anyone else, and the proximity of her firm limbs pressed up against him had him distracted beyond measure.

Not the time, not the place.

And now they were in the middle of a battle, albeit one that had taken a time out, with no weapons or any way of communicating. Every instinct of Domik's was screaming at him to get CJ out of there. Now.

"What's it to be?" he repeated, watching as CJ's pupils pulsed with her erratic heartbeat, the dark dots large against her iris as they fought to take in light in the dark space.

She shook her head before burying it against his chest. "Don't make me decide, Dom. Every time people rely on me, they die."

Domik's brows drew together at that statement. "I'm getting you out of here. I promised I'd keep you safe."

They had no power, and the EMP had been strong enough to knock out not only all the vessels in the battle above Earth, but what looked like the power grid on the continent below. There was no guarantee that things would be back up and running on their own before they ran out of oxygen, and they were an easy target should any enterprising Xakul get their weapons systems back online. So there wasn't much choice.

The sudden loss of power had created a brief reprieve. At least there were no more Xakul ships bearing down on them that the autopilot had to avoid.

If they were to get anywhere, Domik had to see if the backup battery was operational. In these pods, there was a protected battery designed for use in case of a solar storm, which could have a similar effect to an EMP. But how to get to it when the two of them were jammed so tightly in the pod?

"CJ?"

"Yeah?" She sniffled, his heart clenching at the thought that she had been crying.

"How far can you move to your right?" If she could press herself against the far side of the pod, she might get access to the panel where the backup battery was located.

"I'm not sure. Do you want me to try?"

He nodded, realizing she was looking away, said, "Yes."

She eased her hips to one side, the glide of her breasts as she wiggled against his chest, sending a shot of heat right to his dick. He bit back a groan and tensed his hands into fists at his sides, sitting his teeth.

Not the time. Not the place.

The reminder didn't seem to make it to his cock, which strained against his flight suit, the length of it an obvious bulge along his thigh. CJ paused and shot a glance up at him, one eyebrow raised, a giggle escaping her.

"Your—"

"I know!" he bit back, tilting his head back and looking anywhere but at CJ.

"I shouldn't laugh, but I can't help it," she said.

"We're in a life and death situation here. And you're laughing?" He scowled at her, knowing he was being unreasonable, but he couldn't seem to stop the words.

"Maybe you should have a chat with your not-so-little friend there about life and death." She smirked, the corners of her eyes crinkling.

Domik sighed. "Just keep moving."

"Like this?" She wiggled again, obviously trying to elicit a reaction from him.

He lifted an eyebrow and scowled at her.

"All right, all right. I get it. The fun is over. Don't tease the big guy about his massive erection." She huffed.

Domik fought to not smile, biting the inside of his cheeks. "You think I have a massive—"

"Oh! Stop it! I'm moving, OK?" she bit out, finally sliding away from him and squeezing her lean body against the edge of the pod.

Focus. You need to get her safely out of here.

He cleared his mind and reached a hand to push on the panel in front of him. There was a small recess inside where a battery, the size of the tablet that was now floating somewhere to his right, was tucked away. He reached in and pulled it out, turning it in his hands. With relief, he noted that the covering that protected it from solar storm damage was still intact.

One thing is going right today, at least.

"Is it OK?" CJ asked, looking at his hands as he unwrapped the battery.

"We'll soon see," he replied, reaching into his pocket for his multi-tool. He flicked the case open on the battery and pulled out the wires that would connect it to the pod.

"Wires? Old school."

"What has education to do with wires?" Domik asked, his head tilted to one side and his heavy brows drawn together.

CJ laughed. "All the super fancy Taurean tech and I expect everything to be wireless, you know?"

Domik shook his head and huffed out a breath before turning back to the wires separating the ones he needed from the mass and attaching them to the battery. "Sometimes the easiest way is the oldest. What you call fancy," he paused over the pronunciation of the word, making the 'c' sound more like a 'z', then shook his head, "if it works, why change it?"

He cleared his throat and focused on securing the wires before pressing a button on the side of the battery, hoping that the circuitry would connect.

"That's it?" CJ asked, tilting her head to one side as she watched Domik set the battery back in the recess.

"No." Domik prized off another panel, this time to flick a switch.

"Well, don't hold me in suspense, Dom." The slight irritation in her voice was music to his ears. At least she wasn't afraid anymore. He couldn't stand her being afraid. Not CJ, who had been nothing but a small pocket of fire and cheeky comments since the first day she had blown like a wind storm into his life.

Nothing had been the same since.

"The pod needs to do systems checks and a full reset before it will start back up again. That shouldn't take too long, maybe a few minutes." He shrugged, then tapped the panel near his right arm. CJ needing to crane her neck around him to see what he was pointing at. "See that?" he asked, distracted by the brush of her breast against his left arm.

"What am I looking at?" She braced her hand on his bicep and he couldn't help the reflexive flex of the muscle as her delicate fingers gripped his arm.

He stared at her, the tousled blond of her hair speckled with specs of ash, the short strands moving with every one of his breaths. She was so close. He lifted a hand to see if the strand was as silky as they appeared, but stilled, his hand in mid-air, when she spoke.

"Dom?"

He dropped his hand and looked away. "The lights on the panel."

"Oh! I missed them. They were so faint. Does this mean the pod has power again?"

Domik nodded. "I need to override the autopilot and change to manual."

"If it's working again, can't we just set the autopilot and go back to the Zataras?"

"No."

CJ crossed her arms. "Why not?"

Domik gestured out the window of the pod, at the Xakul and Taurean ships that were still scattered, lifeless between them and the great hulking mass of the Zataras that they could now see in the far distance.

On the face of it, what CJ proposed made sense. Just set the thing and go back. But if they had got their pod going, it was only a matter of time before the Xakul ships were up and running, and the cloak was out. And the pod was completely bereft of any weapons.

"See what lies between us and the Zataras?"

CJ nodded.

"What if they get their weapons up?"

She paled at his words. "I see."

"And we don't have any way of communicating."

The communications equipment and the sole tablet they had was also fried, with no chance of recovery. Added to the fact that the autopilot was most likely corrupted, and he couldn't risk it.

As they watched, lights lit up along the side of one of the Xakul ships nearest them, others following. None of the Taurean ships' cloaks were operational, and they were still heavily outnumbered.

Domik cursed, turning back to the pod's manual controls.

CJ stared, openmouthed, as a Xakul ship opened fire on a completely defenseless Taurean ship, which split into two, sending debris flying away from the wreck. A series of escape pods ejected from the wreckage, the Xakul ship picking them off one-by-one.

CJ gasped, grabbing onto Domik's arm.

While they had been in the pod, it had drifted further away from the mass of ships involved in the space battle. They were now right on the edge of the field of debris and ships. There was nothing to get in their way of descent to the planet's surface.

"Let's get the fuck out of here!" CJ forced a laugh as she spoke, lifting her fist to punch him lightly on the arm.

Domik nodded, quickly getting to work.

The pod jerked as he engaged the controls.

"I'm a sound pilot, but I'm nothing like T'arq," he said in apology as the pod continued its jerky descent toward the planet's surface.

"I don't care! Just get us out of here!" CJ cried, clutching at Domik's flight suit with frantic hands.

Within a few minutes he had set up a pseudo-manual control of the pod, and set a heading for the planet below. More of the continent was now in view below them, and Domik aimed the shuttle toward the mass of land.

"That looks like North America," CJ mused, peering out the window of the pod. "Is this pod going to be ok? Will it make it through the atmosphere?"

Domik scoffed. "These things are made to withstand a much more violent descent than what we'll experience."

That's if we make it out of here without damage to the exterior of the pod.

He didn't express his concerns to CJ, thinking it better to keep them to himself, and instead pushed the little pod as fast as it could go. The pod shook as they were hit with debris from the battle, and he automatically tightened his arms around her.

"Oh god. Oh god." She closed her eyes and gripped the fabric of his shirt.

Without realizing, he murmured soothing words, rubbing her back and kissing the top of her head.

The pod continued to shake and shudder as they descended to the planet's surface, the little pod having none of the artificial gravity stabilizers of the larger and more advanced vessels. This pod was a single use, one-way ticket to safety.

As they hurtled towards Earth, the noise in the pod became almost unbearable. He couldn't hear CJ, but he could see her lips moving. Domik was gripped with a sudden terror. What if the pod broke up before they reached safety?

They rocketed closer and closer to the surface, the brief view through the small window in the door showing the blue of the ocean and then the green of land, as the pod rolled over and over. As they picked up speed, the pod shook and rattled, and the noise became so great he couldn't hear CJ's scream as she bounced against the side of the tiny vessel.

The seat he had ripped out had had a harness to keep the occupants safe, but he'd had to remove it so they could both fit. Domik grabbed CJ in his arms, pulling her tight against his chest and cradling her head in his hands.

The pod jerked as the descent arrest system deployed the first of the parachutes. Then the second, slowing them considerably. Domik grunted as he braced his feet and shoulders against the pod, trying to prevent CJ from being bashed around inside their little cocoon. The noise abated, and the window outside showed the view had settled. No longer were they spinning uncontrollably.

Domik brushed CJ's hair back from her forehead, a sticky substance coating his fingers. He lifted his hand to see blood. Eyes widening, he pulled back, horrified.

Please let her not be hurt!

"CJ?" he said gently, his stomach lurching as her head

lolled on her shoulders, her eyes shut. He held her gently, cradling her head in his big palm. "Clodagh, wake up!"

He lifted his fingers beneath her nose, tears welling in his eyes as he felt her breath on his fingers.

She's alive!

He pulled her to his chest and cradled her. He could only hold her and hope she would be all right as the pod drifted slowly downwards toward what he hoped would be safety.

CHAPTER EIGHT

CJ

Warmth surrounded her, and she snuggled deeper into the blankets. There was nothing quite like a sleep-in on a weekend morning. The only thing that would make it better would be a steaming hot cup of coffee and a big stack of pancakes drowned in maple syrup.

She smiled, stretching—and jerked awake as pain speared her head. Opening her eyes, CJ winced at the light, closing them again quickly.

"It's OK. I have you." The rumbling voice was familiar, and she relaxed with a small sigh.

"What happened?"

He shifted her to a sitting position, and she opened her eyes a crack, the light not so intense this time. A warm, but firm, presence was at her back.

Domik. I'm leaning against Domik.

She stiffened, but enormous arms came around her from behind and pulled her back against his chest.

70

"Just relax. You hit your head. What do you remember?" His breath ruffled her hair, and she settled back against his chest, her head tucked between two mammoth pectorals.

"There weren't enough pods... I remember the smoke. It was awful," she said, rubbing her eyes at the memory of the stinging smoke.

"Anything else?" His big hand brushed down her arm as if to warm her, and she realized she was shivering.

"It's cold. Where are we?" she asked, looking around.

They were in a strange white tent.

A tent?

"What else do you remember?" he asked as he flicked open a medi-wand that looked like it had seen better days and began moving it over her head. A warm buzzing filled her head, not unpleasant, and the ache in her skull eased.

"Oh, that feels good." She sighed, closing her eyes. "I remember you. You wouldn't leave me behind."

She paused. Why hadn't he left her behind? Everyone else had left her behind. It was the story of her life. She turned to face him, realizing that she was sitting on one of his big, hard thighs, her legs spread wide over his. She felt her face heat.

It's not like he likes you like that... does he?

She almost slipped off his leg in her frantic movements to face him, but he slid an arm around her back to steady her. Weirdly, she didn't feel trapped, just secure and safe. It was a feeling she could get used to. She shook her head.

No. Don't get used to it.

"Why didn't you leave me?" she asked, desperate to know his reasons. "You could have taken the pod yourself, but you didn't."

His mouth fell open, his eyes wide. "I would never leave you."

At his words, a hesitant smile tipped her lips upwards. "Really?"

He doesn't mean it the way you think. He'd do the same for anyone.

"I couldn't leave someone behind. And we both fit. Just." He shrugged as if it was no big deal, and her heart sank.

See? Don't think you're anything special to him.

"How do you feel?" he asked, concern lining his face.

CJ rolled her shoulders before she stood, needing to put some distance between them. Her legs were shaky, and she leaned against the side of the escape pod as she took a steadying breath. "I feel a little lightheaded, but nothing out of the ordinary. I'll be fine." Her head hit the white fabric of what she realized wasn't a tent. "What is this stuff?" She poked at the fabric, watching it billow up and down again.

"The pod's parachute," Domik replied, standing up and tapping a hand to the metal of the pod that he had been leaning against. "One of them, anyway."

CJ turned on her heel, Domik a little too close for her comfort, her boot grinding into hard-packed, grassless dirt, and pulled at the white fabric of the parachute, needing to see where they were. Domik grabbed a handful, quickly lifting it up and away from her.

CJ's arms dropped to her side as she took in the view laid out in front of them.

Home.

She closed her eyes and took in a deep, gulping breath of fresh air. The smell of dirt surrounded her, and she breathed deeply, lifting her hands to the sky that was colored pink and orange with the setting sun.

The ground was covered with wildflowers, spread like a carpet as far as she could see, and she smiled as she watched them sway. CJ bent to pick a handful, tucking them into one of the chest pockets of her flight suit.

Domik watched on, arms crossed over his chest and his usual impassive expression giving nothing away.

CJ threw her head back and laughed before dancing toward him with a flower in her hand. "Let me give you a little bit of happy, big guy." She smiled as she stood on her toes before him, tucking the bloom behind one ear.

CJ stood back, admiring her handiwork with a cocked head. The contrast of the orange flower against his black hair and dark golden-bronze skin was striking. It didn't detract from his raw power. Instead, it seemed to enhance it.

It wasn't fair.

"Right," she said, smoothing her hands down the front of her flight suit. His eyes followed her hands, and she suddenly felt like a thirteen-year-old girl in front of her crush. She felt her cheeks heat, and she shifted from foot to foot. It was as if she didn't know what to do with all her limbs. "So, any idea where we are?"

Domik watched her, before pointing over her shoulder toward the bare hills that surrounded them. In the fading light, she had to squint to see the outlines of buildings near a road. "I was trying to get us close to somewhere I've been before, one of your Space Force bases. But it was hard to do with so little to guide me, and the controls... well, it wasn't my best piloting." Domik shrugged.

"We made it in one piece, Dom. You did great." She smiled and laid a hand on one of his beefy forearms, the muscles rippling under her fingers.

He looked away, clearing his throat. "Let's walk." He bent to pick up a backpack that he must have pulled from the pod while CJ was unconscious, stuffing the medi-wand inside.

CJ removed her hand and nodded, turning and beginning the descent down the slight rise where the pod had landed. For long minutes they walked in silence, Domik slowing his long stride to match hers, making their way through the field of wildflowers toward the road. As darkness descended, the night sky lit up with stars and the occasional bright flash.

At the first one, CJ flinched, leaning closer to Domik. "It's something burning up as it makes its way through the atmosphere."

He didn't need to say more. CJ shuddered as she considered the many Xakul and Taurean ships that were battling above them.

More and more flashes lit up the night sky, and suddenly the peace she had felt disappeared.

"We have to stop this," CJ said, breaking the silence that had spread as they walked.

Domik's reply, when it came, was short and to the point. "We need to get to the base first."

Suddenly, it all seemed too hard, and CJ's eyes filled with tears. She lifted a hand to rub at her face, and she stumbled as her foot slipped on the loose ground.

Growling, Domik swung her into his arms, one arm under her legs and the other behind her back. CJ looped her arms around his neck and settled against his chest. She didn't protest, knowing that he could walk faster without her struggling beside him.

His heart thudded beneath her cheek, his chest rising and falling with each breath he took. She let her fingers slide underneath the heavy weight of his hair where it slid over his shoulders, having come out of its confining braid—what CJ liked to think of as Domik's battle braids—at some point. His hair was thick and dark, almost entirely black, but with strands of dark bronze spread throughout that she hadn't noticed before.

The fading light shone across his face, casting him in even more of a golden glow than his usual skin tone. He was stunningly, achingly beautiful, and her heart thudded with longing.

She broke her gaze away and stared ahead at the cluster of buildings which suddenly appeared before them. She squinted to see better in the fading light.

"I think that's a gas station," she said as they reached the road and Domik put her back on her feet. She held onto his arm to steady herself before walking toward the buildings. "How far do you think it is?" She turned to ask, casting a sideways look at Domik.

"One of your kilometers, no further," he said confidently, and CJ knew he was right.

"That's not far. It looks pretty quiet." She squinted, trying to see if the buildings were occupied.

"A little too quiet," he said, his tone wary.

They walked together down the road, which cut straight through the valley where they had landed. The ground on either side was low and rocky, with little in the way of vegetation except for the occasional scrubby bush and the carpet of wildflowers. In the distance, the road rose over a hill, behind which the sun was about to disappear.

This would be perfect under different circumstances.

She smiled to herself, Domik casting her a look, one eyebrow raised in question.

"Domik?"

"Hmm?" He barely replied, looking straight ahead to the gas station where they were headed, off to one side of what CJ was thinking of as the highway.

"What's going to happen to us?" she asked, the fear she had been keeping at bay making her voice shake. She looked up at him hopefully, trying to not cry.

What's wrong with me?

He touched her on the shoulder, turning her toward him. "We will make it to the base, and back to the Zataras. It's going to be OK," he whispered.

She nodded, hiccupping, as she swiped at her eyes with the backs of her fingers. "I know it's silly. It's just been a long day."

He squeezed her shoulder gently before letting go. "Let's find somewhere to rest and work out how to get to the base."

She nodded; arms wrapped around her middle against the chill now that the sun had dropped beyond the horizon. "All right."

He turned and began walking again toward the gas station, CJ trotting alongside him. As they approached, the buildings loomed out of the darkness. There was no movement of people or cars, no lights, no noise. It was as if everyone had just up and left.

The few vehicles parked nearby were abandoned, parked haphazardly, doors ajar as if the owners had just stepped out.

All the horror movies she'd ever seen raged into life in the dark. There could be many hidden threats. As they walked closer, she sidled toward Domik and slid her hand into his, needing to feel his strength. He looked down at their hands, fingers entwined, and then up at her.

"So, how are we going to do this?"

There was a front door into the gas station, which they bypassed, instead heading for the rear of the building. There was a small outbuilding to one side with a sign declaring it a mechanic's workshop, and a trailer with an awning attached under which a set of deck chairs was placed.

"So someone lives and works here. But where are they?" CJ mused quietly, conscious of not making too much noise.

Domik let go of her hand and moved to the trailer.

"Be careful," she hissed after him, moving to hide beside an abandoned truck. While Domik was gone, CJ looked inside the truck, finding a shotgun under the rear seat and claiming it with a triumphant fist pump.

A hand on her shoulder had her jumping in fright.

"Shh. It's just me," Domik said, his voice near her ear sending shivers down her spine.

"Fuck me, Dom. You scared the shit out of me." She sighed, closing her eyes and resting her head against the door of the truck. She turned and showed him the gun. "I found us a gun, at least."

He looked from her to the gun in her hands and back again and grunted.

"I know how to use it. Trust me." She raised her eyebrow.

"I do." He lifted the item in his hands for her to see.

"What is it?" It was a matte black colored box, about half the size of a shoebox.

"It's Taurean."

"What?" she gaped as he opened the box, looking up at him with wide eyes.

Domik shifted the box so she could look inside.

"What the fuck?"

CHAPTER NINE

Domik

This was bad. Very bad. Domik shook his head slowly as he pulled the two objects from the box, placing them on the hood of the truck in front of them. He stood back, the hair on the back of his neck prickling as he rubbed his jaw.

"Is that...?" CJ asked in a hushed voice.

"Yes," Domik replied, staring unblinkingly at what was, without any doubt, a Taurean wrist comm and a plasma pistol.

"How...?" CJ looked up at him, not finishing the sentence.

He shook his head. "This can't be a legitimate source."

CJ licked her lips nervously, nodding. "So, who would have access to this kind of equipment on Earth? Apart from Space Force, of course." She waved her arm around the abandoned gas station. "Because I don't think this has anything to do with them."

Domik nodded. "No, it doesn't."

He scooped up the wrist comm and strapped it to his arm

before pocketing the plasma pistol. His own had been lost in the escape from the shuttle, and the reassuring weight of the pistol back in his thigh holster settled him somewhat.

The plan hadn't changed. They needed to get to the Space Force base and somehow tell Taurean command about what they had discovered. But the niggling thought plagued him. What if there were more than just this one stash? It had been abandoned, suggesting that the people here had left in a hurry and had considered one pistol and one comm disposable.

The thought sobered him.

"Let's see if we can figure out where we are," Domik said, gesturing toward the dark gas station.

"Can't you just use the comm?" CJ asked, brows wrinkled in confusion.

Domik shook his head. "I tried already. It doesn't work."

"The EMP?" she asked.

"Most likely," he said. He might get it working again, but it was doubtful. The EMP had fried his own wrist comm, along with CJ's. He'd tried to fix them but didn't have the delicate tools, so he'd destroyed them instead so they wouldn't fall into the wrong hands. He explained as much to CJ, who nodded.

"Let's check out the gas station," he said, gesturing toward the building with his head. "I'll go first, follow me, and stay out of sight. Just in case."

He didn't mention in case of what, but by CJ's nod and her grim expression, he didn't need to. He felt a sudden swell of pride at how well she had handled the events of the last few hours. She had been terrified, and yet she had focused and kept calm. Domik scanned the back entry of the gas station, preferring this way rather than the glass covered front. He pulled the plasma pistol from his holster and, holding it ready, considered the best way to approach. There was no light coming from inside and, as he approached the back door, nothing moved.

The door was unlocked, and he pressed the handle down slowly, and prized it open enough to slide through. A slight creak from the hinges made him grimace and pause, but no noise or movement came from the darkened interior.

When CJ had followed him, she shut the door slowly, propping it open with a wedge of wood that must have been left there for just that purpose. They were in a hallway, the end of which opened onto the shop floor. To the right, a door opened into an office, a mess of papers spread over a battered wooden desk. A stack of crates in the corner held cleaning products and rolls of paper towel.

Domik gave them a cursory look before moving on. To the left a second door opened into a bathroom, Domik's nose wrinkling at the smell.

They could have used some of those cleaners in here.

CJ gave a slight cough as she caught a whiff of the bathroom, and Domik suppressed a smile.

As they approached the main shop floor, Domik held up a hand to stop CJ behind him. He gestured for her to stay put and hurried along the back wall, checking between the racks of products on display.

When he was satisfied that they were alone, he returned to where CJ was pressed against the wall where he'd left her, looking in the opposite direction. He reached out to touch her shoulder, and she jolted and let out a shriek of fright.

"Shit! You scared me. How do you move so quietly? It's unnatural." She rubbed a hand over her face.

He lifted one shoulder in apology, and she laughed nervously.

"This is like every bad horror movie, you know?" She released a shaky breath. "Right. Let's see what we can find out."

They walked toward the front counter, where a rack had a display of pamphlets.

"Oooh! I remember these!" CJ grabbed one of them and opened it. "Huh. That makes sense." She pored over the writing on the page, before lifting it to show him.

Domik leaned over her shoulder to see, but the words made no sense to him. "I can't read that."

"Oh, I forgot," she said with an apologetic smile. "Right, so we're here." She pointed a finger at a spot on a map in the center of the page. "We're near a place called Death Valley, actually not that far from the base where we want to go, which is around here." She stabbed her finger at a second spot on the map.

"Death Valley?"

That sounds ominous.

"Oh, it's just a name." She smiled up at him, and his breath caught.

She is so beautiful.

Domik grunted and turned away, walking toward a rack of clothing and flipping through mindlessly. CJ approached and stilled his hands with one of her own. "Different clothing is a good idea, but I don't think that what you're looking through is going to work."

"Huh? Why not?"

She gave him a look that said, 'just trust me on this', before pulling out a violently pink top that looked far too small for him.

"Oh," he said, looking down as she held it up to his chest with a giggle.

"The map shows a town not far away, with a motel and a department store. Let's see if we can get a ride and head over there."

She tossed the pink monstrosity back on the rack and turned, hands on hips, to look around.

"But first, let's eat something. I'm starved." She rubbed her stomach as it rumbled. "And I have a hankering for some junk food."

For the next few minutes, Domik trailed CJ around the shop holding a basket that she placed anything and everything she wanted into. When the basket was full, she took it from him and led him outside to a table and chairs at the front of the store.

She began pulling the food from the basket and opening packets with an exclamation of glee.

"I have missed you so much," she said, much to Domik's amusement, as she bit into what smelled like pure sugar but looked like a fluffy cloud. CJ closed her eyes and moaned as she chewed, a little dusting of powdered sugar on the corner of her lip drawing Domik's eyes like a beacon.

Are those lips as soft as they look?

He looked away and absently opened a bottle of what CJ had confirmed was water, taking a deep swallow. Picking up a packet at random, he opened it to find most of it air. He reached in and picked out a roughly circular, pale yellow shape. Lightweight and very delicate, it crushed a little under his fingers.

Domik looked from the supposed food to CJ, who nodded encouragingly, so he popped it in his mouth and bit down. The flavor was... strange. Salt and air, but not much else.

"Do you like it?" CJ asked. Domik couldn't bear to disappoint her, so he nodded and was rewarded with a beaming smile.

Ah, Clodagh. I would eat cardboard and call it gourmet, as long as you smiled at me like that.

Domik ate another of what CJ told him were potato chips, deciding they weren't awful, but weren't exactly his favorite thing to eat either. Rinsing down the last of the packet with the bottle of water, he stood up and strode across the front of the gas station toward a series of parked vehicles.

"Where do you think they all went?" CJ asked, trotting along behind him with a bottle of water in one hand and another sugary food item in the other. If she liked those foods so much, he would make sure she always had them available.

"What is that?" He pointed at the packet in her hand, wanting to know what it was so he could buy more for her.

"This?" she asked, lifting it up to look at the small packet with a grin.

"Yes. What is it?"

"A cake of sorts. It's called a Twinkie. I know they're terrible for me, but I haven't had one in so long that I just went a little overboard." She frowned as she looked at it. "I probably shouldn't eat this one, or I'll make myself sick." She went to toss it aside, but Domik grabbed her hand to stop her.

"Keep it. You can have it later." He wasn't about to let her get rid of something that made her so happy.

"OK," she said, dragging the two syllables out.

He nodded. Glad that she understood. He faced the vehicles that were parked on one side of the gas station. There was another truck, like the one to the rear of the building, a smaller vehicle and a curious looking four-wheeled vehicle that looked very similar to the speeders that he had used on Taurus.

"I think we have a problem," CJ said as she looked him up and down and then gestured at the smaller vehicle. "There's no way you're fitting in that."

"What about the speeder?" Domik said, pointing at the four-wheeled vehicle.

CJ's eyebrows shot up and her mouth dropped open. "You have those on Taurus? We call them quads."

"Quads?" He stepped closer to the four-wheeled vehicle, strolling around it. It looked old, but in good condition. There was space for both of them, with a crate on the back for storage that had him nodding in satisfaction. At least this way CJ would be nicely secured in front of the crate.

"As in quad bikes; a kind of motorbike, but with four wheels."

Domik turned to her and held out his hand. "Come on."

She hesitated, looking at his outstretched hand for a long moment. "Do you know how to ride one of those?"

Domik shrugged. "No, but I've ridden speeders and they seem similar."

CJ pursed her lips before speaking hesitantly. "I don't know, Dom. It seems pretty dangerous."

"More dangerous than crash landing in an escape pod?"

CJ's lips twitched. "OK. You have me there."

"Let me see if I can get it started." Domik turned to the

quad and waved a hand over what seemed to be the control panel.

A burst of laughter sounded, and then CJ shouldered past him to reach between the handlebars. "This is the key. It needs to be turned. And the bike should be in neutral when you start it, or it's going to stall."

Domik nodded to her. "Why don't you drive it?"

"Me?" She looked at him in shock.

"Why not?" Domik didn't see what the problem was. She obviously knew something about them, and it wasn't as if they had far to travel.

"Um..." She looked at the bike. "All right, let me see if I can get it started."

Domik watched as she turned the key and kicked the machine into life.

"Oh! I didn't think it would start!" she yelled over the noise of the engine.

Most Earth vehicles, from what he had read, were electric. But there were still some older vehicles that relied on petrol to run. Those would be the ones least likely to have been impacted by the EMP, and one reason Domik had chosen this one.

Domik shook his head slightly. "It's too old to be electric." He lifted a leg to slide on over the back of the seat behind CJ, the frame of the bike dropping with his added weight.

CJ slid forward as far as she could go, her legs on either side of the bike's fuel tank, but Domik reached an arm forward to wrap around her middle and pull her back slightly into the vee between his legs.

"Let's go," he said, pointing in the opposite direction to where they had landed in the pod.

CJ nodded and, with a lurch that had Domik reaching one arm back to steady himself, they were on their way.

The noise of the engine was soon overcome by the wind whipping past as CJ tuned the bike onto the highway and opened the throttle. With a whoop, she smiled and turned her head to smile at Domik quickly, before facing back up the road.

Any of his hair that had remained pulled back whipped loose quickly, flying around his head as they sped along the dark road. The headlight from the bike was the only light, apart from that of the stars.

CHAPTER TEN

CJ

Domik's presence behind her on the bike was reassuring. His solid frame warm at her back as the chilly night air whipped at her clothing. They quickly crested the hills they had seen from the gas station, and she paused the bike at the top of the rise.

"There should be a town down there," she said, twisting on the seat to look at Domik.

Oh, wow.

Her eyes widened as she took in his disheveled state. His hair, that was usually pulled back in a thick braid that fell down his back, was loose around his shoulders. The thick strands having been whipped into a halo of black, giving him a dark and dangerous appearance when added with the shaved sides of his head.

He looks like a Viking.

CJ licked her lips and swallowed, her eyes dropping to his

mouth. Barely registering that he had said something, she blinked. "Sorry, I missed that."

Domik barely raised an eyebrow. "The EMP may have been powerful enough to knock out an entire continent."

"Oh," CJ said. Turning back to look at the town below.

Domik reached past and flicked the headlight off. "Let's not draw too much attention to ourselves."

CJ nodded, letting off the brake and letting the bike roll slowly down the hill. She moved to the side of the road, seeking the shelter of the scrubby bushes to not appear so obvious against the hill.

When they were approaching the outskirts of town, Domik pointed to a dirt track that ran off to one side of the road, and CJ pulled the bike off the road and parked it under a tree, out of sight. She turned off the ignition, and they dismounted.

Grabbing a bottle of water that he had stashed in the crate on the back, CJ took a swig and capped the bottle, tucking it into a pocket on the outside of her pants.

The motel was not large, comprising one long, rectangular brick building over one level. There was a big sign that would normally have been lit up in neon lights, eerie in darkness. There were no cars parked outside the rooms, the motel appearing completely abandoned.

CJ waited near the front of the building as Domik checked through the windows of the rooms, confirming there was no one about, before opening the door to the reception area. This time she waited outside until he reappeared to tell her it was clear.

A beam of light from a torch Domik had found behind the counter lit up the room, and she blinked to clear her vision. Whoever had decorated the reception area liked purple. A lot. Everything was purple, from the counter to the threadbare carpet under her feet. CJ blinked as she stood and turned on the spot. Even the walls were purple.

"It's very..." she trailed off, lacking the words.

"Purple," Domik supplied, one side of his mouth lifting.

Was that an actual dimple?

CJ froze, feeling bereft as the deliciously sexy dimple disappeared.

"No," she murmured. Months. It had taken months to just get a lift of his lips. Not even a full smile and he had a goddamned dimple hiding all this time?

"It is purple," Domik said, gesturing at the walls.

CJ shook her head and, skirting the counter, perused the board where a series of keys were hanging. No swipe cards for this motel, old school keys.

Well, at least the locks will work. I hope.

"Which room do you want, Dom?" she asked, reading the names printed in block letters on the plastic tags on which each of the keys hung. "Oh boy. You have a choice of—I really wish I had could make a drumroll here—the Daytona room." She grimaced, imagining just what would be in that room. More power to motor sport fans, but a racecar bed was not her idea of fun. She dropped that key tag and moving onto the next one, "the Blue Suede room, a couple that I don't think we should go anywhere near with a barge pole, and... oh, this one seems like it could be actually OK. The room with a view."

Grabbing the last key, she lifted it off the hook and turned to face Domik. "I don't want to be alone, so you're coming with me, big boy." She winked, faking a confidence she didn't have.

Domik just grunted and followed her from the reception room and along the walkway until they reached the room. "I don't see what the view would be—"

As CJ opened the door and let it swing inside, they both stopped, mouths agape.

"Oh, boy. Trust us to end up in some kind of sex motel." CJ laughed, swiping at her eyes with the back of her hand.

They stepped into the room, Domik ducking to not hit his head on the door frame. Turning around, she took in what had to be the most mirrors she had ever seen in one room. They were behind the bed, which was draped in a leopard print coverlet. Looking up, CJ snorted at the mirror on the ceiling.

Domik slowly shut the door with one hand, staring transfixed at the mirrors above the bed.

"I don't want to know what kind of stuff has gone on in here, but I really need a shower." She pointed at the leopard print coverlet that had seen better days. "I'm going to hope this is clean."

She walked toward the bathroom and laughed. "Dom!"

He raced into the room after her, and suddenly it felt as if they were back in the escape pod. They were crowded in close together, with barely enough room to turn around.

"What's wrong?" He asked, staring around the room with his plasma pistol at the ready.

"Nothing. Well, except for this crime against interior decorating," she gestured at the walls, which, unsurprisingly, were covered with mirrors.

"Oh. Now I understand," Domik said, holstering his pistol. "You're the view."

CJ's breath caught as she stared up at him, hands braced against the bench behind her. There didn't seem to be enough room in this bathroom for the two of them, something which Domik seemed to realize a few seconds later, backing out of the room.

He bumped his head on the door frame and, mumbling an apology, lifted a hand to rub it as CJ grimaced in sympathy. "I'll just... wait." He mumbled and left, shutting the door behind him.

The door opened again quickly, a large bronzed hand thrusting the torch at her.

"Thank you." She took the torch and placed it on the floor so the light shone on the ceiling, lighting up the room.

What was that all about?

CJ looked at the closed bathroom door in confusion. It was almost as if he had felt the same attraction to her and been uncomfortable in the space.

But no, he couldn't... could he?

Shaking her head, she quickly undressed, piling her clothes on the floor near the door.

The room had been made up ready for the next guests, so there were towels and soap, which she sighed in relief at seeing.

There was a spa bath with a shower over the top, around the edges lined with those mirrors, and she stepped into the spa to turn the shower on. Bracing herself for cold water, she was pleasantly surprised to find there was hot available, steam filling the room and fogging the mirrors.

CJ quickly lathered the soap and scrubbed her skin,

ridding herself of all the ash and dirt that had caked her skin. She quickly rinsed, not knowing how long the hot water would last and wanting to leave some for Domik.

Stepping out of the shower, she wiped the steam away from the mirror and stood naked, looking at herself for the first time in a long time. She wasn't one to stare at herself in the mirror, and on the Zataras she had so little time between missions that she just crashed when she got to her room. And you could forget about looking in the mirror in the gym change rooms. She was more interested in getting in the shower than staring at herself in the mirror.

So it was with fresh eyes that she surveyed her naked form. She was pale from spending so little time in the sun, her tan lines from the one week she'd spent on a Taurean beach during leave now faded to barely nothing.

Dropping the towel to the floor, she turned one way, then the other, casting a critical eye over her muscled body.

As a teenager she had hoped for breasts how some girls hoped for a pony, jealously looking on while her friends gained the attention of boys. As she grew older and her chest barely increased, she realized that smaller boobs were sometimes a benefit. She barely had to wear a bra, her sports crop giving enough support during exercise.

CJ ran her hands down her sides, tracing her fingers over her taut stomach and over the slight flare of her hips. She turned side on, cocking her head to one side as she assessed the swell of her ass. She might not have much in the breast department, but she sure had an ass that didn't quit.

She gave a short chuckle, turning away from the mirror to hang her towel over the rack and grab a toothbrush from the cup on the bench and clean her teeth.

When she was finished, she eyed her filthy clothes on the floor and wrinkled her nose. She did not want to put those back on. Not now that she was clean.

Padding the few steps to the door in her bare feet, she opened it a crack and peered out. "Dom?"

A shifting of shadows was all the notice she had that he had moved, and she gasped as he appeared in front of the door, his huge body lit by the faint vertical beam of light from the bathroom behind her.

His dark eyes glowed in the light, and her breath caught as she tipped her head back to look up at him.

"Uh. Towel?"

Oh, dear god. Forget how to speak, much?

She groaned inwardly before clearing her throat and trying again. "Is there another towel? My clothes are filthy and..." she trailed off as he turned to the bed and bent, his pants pulling tight over taut ass cheeks.

Fuck. That's one tight ass.

He cleared his throat, and she realized she had been staring. Her cheeks flushed, and she looked away. "Here," he said, handing her another towel, which she took with a nod of thanks before shutting the bathroom door and wrapping it around her.

She opened the door again, stepping out into the much cooler motel room. Domik had moved as far away as he could get from the bathroom, leaning against the wall near the door to the parking lot outside.

CJ gripped the towel tightly, pulling it closer like a protective shield, before sitting on the edge of the bed, her back to Domik.

A quiet click was the only sign that Domik had left the room.

She turned, mouth agape, to look at the closed door.

He'd left? I can't be that awful to look at, surely?

She sighed and flopped back on the bed, staring at the ceiling in the flickering light of the torch. Her thoughts quickly turned to the team. Had they all made it safely back to the Zataras? She felt sick with worry, but there was nothing she could do about it now.

She rubbed her arms against the night chill, wishing that she had something more to wear than her filthy uniform and a towel.

A click of the door shutting had CJ jolting upright in fright, grabbing the towel with one hand as she stood and turned to see Domik had returned, with a lumpy bundle in his arms.

"What is that?" she said, curiosity winning out over her fright.

He dropped the bundle onto the bed. "Clothes. Something might fit."

She looked from the pile of clothes to Domik and back. "How?"

He shrugged. "There was a room for washing clothes behind the reception area." He gestured at the pile. "See if there's something you like. I need to get clean."

He walked to the door and checked the lock before entering the bathroom. CJ tried to ignore that he left the door open, a flash of a bronzed ass as he pulled his pants off having her spin away, calling over her shoulder, "You can shut the door."

He didn't reply. The sounds of running water as he turned the shower on, telling her all she needed to know about that. She busied herself sorting through the pile of clothes on the bed, pulling out a pair of black athletic leggings and holding them up. Deciding they might fit, she put them to one side. There were some tee shirts that might do to sleep in, being too big for CJ but far too small for Domik, and she added this to the pile.

She picked up one of the oversized tee shirts, shooting a look at the bathroom door to make sure Domik was out of sight before slipping it over her head.

The sound of water running stopped and a masculine groan hit her just as she had the shirt over her head, startling her enough that her towel slipped, leaving her standing naked with a tee-shirt over her head.

Oh fuck. Please tell me he's not looking.

CHAPTER ELEVEN

Domik

Despite being so tall that he almost hit his head on the bathroom ceiling, he enjoyed the shower. Hot water beat down on his back from the shower rose. Grabbing one of the floral scented bottles, he looked at it suspiciously before shrugging and squirting the liquid into his hand.

He reached up and lathered his hair, running his hands through the long strands.

He couldn't remember the last time he'd had a proper haircut. Every few weeks, he took to the sides with clippers, preferring the shorn feeling around his ears. The long, dark top part he braided tightly to his head to not get in the way during battle, but now it hung loose and wet, reaching part way down his back.

CJ's hair was the opposite of his, short and blond, whereas his was long and dark. He wondered if hers was as soft as it looked. He bent to rinse the soap from his hair and lathered his skin, running his hands over his thickly muscled arms.

Do I appear monstrous to her?

Domik knew he was inhumanly large, standing head and shoulders over even the tallest of the humans—man or woman. CJ didn't even reach his shoulder, and she towered over Krystal, who was the smallest human Domik had met.

He cut the water off and stepped out of the shower, groaning as he reached for a towel that wasn't there. In the rush to get away from CJ, showing far too much skin in her own tiny towel, he had left it in the bedroom.

He heard a gasp from the bedroom and spun to look through the open door. He froze. CJ was standing with her back to him. Her towel pooled around her feet. Naked.

Well, almost naked. She was dressing, and he should look away, but he was transfixed. The light from the torch danced across her skin, lighting the swell of her ass and casting shadows across the dip of her spine. Two little dimples at the base of her spine drew his eyes.

She was gorgeous.

His cock swelled at the sight of her exposed skin; the lean length of her legs graceful as she frantically shifted from foot to foot.

"Fuck," she said, struggling with whatever it was she was trying to don.

What is that?

Domik could no more watch her struggle than he could have abandoned her on the spaceship to die. Before he knew what he was about, he strode into the room and lifted the shirt up.

"What are you doing?" She gasped, throwing her hands

over her naked body and glaring at him over her shoulder as she curled over herself, trying to hide from him.

As if those hands could hide all that he found enticing. He chuckled, forgetting for a moment his promise to not smile, one side of his lips tilting in a grin.

She froze, staring at his lips, and he pressed them together.

"Twice," she breathed, still staring at his mouth. "That's twice you've smiled."

He shook his head, one eyebrow lifted. "That wasn't a smile."

"Oh, yes it was." She smirked then, remembering she was naked, scowled again. "Give me that." She made a grab for the shirt.

Domik held it open and lifted it over her head. "Arms up."

She glared at him again, but turned her back and did as he asked. Domik slowly lowered the shirt over her hands, closing his eyes and breathing in her scent.

She smelled like clean woman. Like peace and contentment. She smelled like home.

He snapped his eyes open.

You're everything to me, Clodagh. But what am I to you?

Her head appeared through the neck hole of the garment, slipping to bare one shoulder, the hem settling around her mid-thigh. She tugged at the hem, but turned to look at him. "You're soaking wet."

He looked down at his chest, and she followed his gaze, gasping as she caught sight of his now straining cock. Domik was not ashamed of his nudity, but going by her reaction, thought it best to cover up. He bent down to grab the towel that she had dropped, still pooled around her feet. He paused as he grabbed it and looked up at her. "I forgot a towel."

She nodded. "Ah, yes... you did." She swallowed, jerking her eyes away to stare up and over his shoulder, unfocused.

He stood, holding the towel in front of him to hide his now almost fully engorged dick, the heavy weight of it bouncing as he stood. He pushed it against his stomach, sticky pre cum leaking onto the towel. Turning to return to the bathroom to give CJ some space, her hand gripped his forearm. He looked down; her neat nails little half-moons on his bronzed skin.

"I think these might fit you," she said, grabbing something from the bed and thrusting it at him. He took it from her and nodded his thanks before retreating into the bathroom, this time shutting the door behind him.

He quickly dried himself, toweling his hair and leaving it loose around his shoulders to dry. He then looked at the clothing she had handed him, holding them up. They were pants of a soft gray fabric. He shrugged and pulled them on, the fabric straining around his thighs, the waistband dipping low on his hips.

At least they're comfortable.

He picked up the torch and opened the door, the beam of light from the torch shining in a long line against the very pink carpet.

Humans have very odd taste.

CJ was sitting on the bed, looking tiny, with her knees drawn up to her chest and the big tee-shirt pulled down over her legs. Her feet peeked out from the bottom of the fabric, her head lifting from where it had been resting on her knees.

She blinked at him, eyes widening and mouth dropping open as she stared.

Domik looked down at himself, and then back up at her. "What?"

She squeaked, then cleared her throat before continuing. "Uh, nothing. Nothing at all," she said in a rush, before sliding her legs free and jumping up from the bed. She backed away against the wall, her hands flat against the mirrored surface.

Domik could see himself in the mirror behind her, the contrast between their sizes stark. The shadows from the dim light gave him a menacing appearance, and he turned away.

It was bad enough that he was so huge; he didn't want to frighten her. But she knew he wouldn't hurt her, didn't she?

You let no one truly know you, though.

He shook his head, the dark locks shaking slightly as he turned away.

"Those pants..." CJ's voice was soft in the dark room as she trailed off.

"What about them?" He said over his shoulder, bending to open a cupboard door below what looked like a view screen attached to the one of the few walls that wasn't covered in mirrors.

"They don't really fit."

Domik stood and turned toward her, tugging at the fabric that had stretched to its maximum around his legs. "Is there anything else?"

"No."

"Should I go naked?"

"No!"

The trials of the day, being alone with CJ... he wasn't sure exactly what possessed him to ask his next question. "The idea of me naked is that bad?"

She blanched, shaking her head slowly as he took a single step toward her.

"No, it isn't? Or no it is?"

She swallowed. "Um..."

Domik let the smile he had been holding back for what felt like months lift his lips slowly. She was so adorably discombobulated that he couldn't help it.

"Don't worry, Clodagh. I'm not going to strip naked and wave my dick around." He laughed at the thought.

She blinked at him. "Oh."

His smile dropped as he stared at her in consideration.

Why did she sound disappointed?

He took another step closer across the small room, bringing her just outside of arm's reach. His arms, not her much shorter ones. She would have to step toward him to touch him.

When he spoke, his voice was low, almost a growl. "Are you disappointed?"

Her eyes were enormous as she licked her lips nervously and stared up at him. "Maybe." She whispered.

He shifted forward, ever so slightly, and tilted his head toward her. "What did you say?"

She looked down at the floor, as if trying to hide. "Maybe I am disappointed."

He reached one finger to gently tip her head up to look at him. "Tell me what you want, Clodagh."

She shivered, but didn't look away. One breath, then two. Another. Just when Domik thought she wouldn't be brave enough to say what she wanted, she lifted her chin, pulled her shoulders back and spoke. Her voice was clear and steady as she said words he never expected to hear from her.

"I want you to hold me, Dom."

He went immediately rigid, his cock straining at the tight fabric of his pants, tenting them almost obscenely. He shifted, adjusting the heavy weight with one hand to fit more comfortably, but stalling with his hand still on his cock as she watched.

A thrill raced through him at the thought of her watching him. He cupped his thick length, watching her. Her breath was coming in short bursts, her hands twisting in the fabric of her tee-shirt, the hem riding up to show more of her legs than he thought she meant to.

Sliding his hand down, he caressed his heavy balls, groaning at the sensation.

Her eyes shot to his. "Dom?"

"Yes?"

"I need to feel like I'm not alone. That's all."

His hand stilled. If that's what she wanted, then that's what he would do. He removed his hand and gripped her shoulders gently. His hands were so big that his thumbs touched at the front of her throat, across her collarbones, and his fingers still curled over the back of her shoulders.

She closed her eyes, her head falling backward, exposing her throat.

Domik bent, his head dipping to slide his nose along the pale column of her neck. She tilted her head to one side as he breathed in her scent. Warm, clean woman, and the scent all of her own. The feeling of being home hit him again. He pushed it aside.

Maybe not forever. But maybe you can pretend?

He gathered her in his arms and dropped a kiss to the top of her head. "I want to make you feel good," he said against her hair.

She pulled away slightly to look at him. "Then hold me." She smiled, lifting a hand to rest on his bare chest over his heart, which thudded so fast he swore she could hear it.

Don't let her guess how much I want her.

Her hand burned like a brand where it touched him, and he covered it with one of his.

She opened her mouth to speak, but squeaked as the room was plunged into darkness. "Oh, shit! The torch!" She laughed.

He released her and stepped sideways just as she did, CJ colliding into his chest, her arms pressed against him. His hands went automatically around her, her slight figure fitting against him as if they were made for each other.

"Hold on, Dom. I think I saw some candles somewhere..." She slipped out of his arms, moving around him in the room.

His eyes adjusted quickly to the darkness, the faint moonlight sending her into relief as she walked in front of the windows that were covered only with a filmy curtain. A spark of a match and then a flare of light, the smell of sulfur hitting his nostrils. CJ's face was lit by a glow of a small candle, which was quickly followed by a handful of others.

She walked around to his side of the bed, lighting another few candles and placing them on the small side table.

The glow lit the room in a soft, flickering light that danced across her skin, lighting her in a soft hue. His breath caught as she turned and smiled at him.

"That's better," she said. She bit her lip as she looked up at him, uncertainty in her expression.

Domik lifted an eyebrow and held out his hand to her. The choice had to be hers.

She looked at his hand, chewing on her lip. "Could you go back to the way things were? After this, I mean."

The way things were? Being tortured every day by her presence and not being able to touch her, to hold her, to comfort her when she was upset or afraid? If in his whole life all he had was this one night, then it would have to be enough.

He looked at her uncertain expression, and hating himself for it, he lied. "Yes, I can go back to the way things were."

She smiled a little and slid her hand into his.

CHAPTER TWELVE

CJ

H er hand was tiny compared to his. Long fingers slid around hers, tugging her gently toward him.

How stupid could she be? Going back to the way things were? She never looked back, that way only lay heartbreak. She should know better.

But right now? Right now, she didn't care. She needed him like she needed air to breathe. And so she stamped down any doubts, pushing them aside and let herself be pulled into his arms.

"Dom?" She looked up at him, spreading her hands over his chest to loop around his neck.

"Yes?" She felt the deep rumble of his voice through his chest. Dear gods, he was huge! She had always known that he was big, but there was knowing and then there was being pressed up against the sheer wall of muscle that was his body.

"Get into bed." She ordered, surprised at herself.

Domik smirked, that single dimple appearing once more to tease her with its presence before disappearing from sight as he mock frowned at her, a teasing glint in his eyes. "Not before you."

She stepped back, climbing onto the bed and crawling on hands and knees to the center, knowing that the hem was riding up and giving him a glimpse of her naked ass.

A choked noise from behind her confirmed her suspicion, and she giggled.

He gripped both her ankles in one huge hand and dragged her backward, her stomach hitting the bed and the tee-shirt riding up to the middle of her back, her legs pressed together.

"You want to give me orders?" One of his enormous hands was still wrapped around her ankles, his thumb stroking her skin lazily as lowered himself to kneel on the bed behind her.

CJ shook her head slowly as she watched him over her shoulder, kneeling above her, those gray sweatpants riding so low on his hips she could see a shadow near the deep v where his abdominal muscles dipped into the waistband. She could not look away as he slid one hand inside his pants.

Holy fucking shit. He's stroking himself.

She was mesmerized as his hand slid down his length, hidden by the fabric of his pants. She licked her lips and went to roll over, but his hand held fast, pushing her feet gently but insistently into the mattress.

"Clodagh?" Her name was like a purr, his voice deep and sensual as it flowed over her. "I won't do anything you are not fully consenting to. If you say stop, I'll stop."

She breathed a sigh of relief. "All right."

"Good," he said, his hand pulling free of his pants, the elastic hitting his washboard stomach with a snap.

CJ's face flamed, and she buried it in her hands as she lay face down on the bed. The cool night air kissed her naked skin, and she was achingly aware of how exposed she was with Domik kneeling behind her while she wore no panties.

He slid his hands slowly up her calves, thumbs moving in circles, kneading knots she didn't know she had. She moaned, dropping her hands to her sides and letting herself sink, bonelessly, into the mattress.

His hands slid further up her legs, thumbs brushing over the backs of her thighs to where her legs met her ass. He ran his thumbs tantalizingly close to her center, and she shifted her hips, trying to get closer.

Domik's hands stilled on her ass, his thumbs touching near the base of her spine and his fingers reaching to her hips, before moving away to more neutral territory. His hands kneaded and soothed. When he reached her tee-shirt, he pushed it up gently and slid his hands underneath to grip her shoulders.

She should feel more exposed, lying here almost naked, but she didn't.

Domik shifted to straddle her legs, keeping his weight off her as he sat back on his heels. CJ lifted onto her forearms and turned to look at him over her shoulder. "Everything OK?" she asked. His unreadable gaze trailed over her naked back, his hands resting on his thick thighs.

He nodded, waving a finger in a lazy circle to show she should lie back down. She suppressed a grin and did as he asked, settling back onto the bed.

She jerked as his warm hands settled on her lower back,

but relaxed as he kneaded and soothed, his strong fingers sending her into a dreamy state of relaxation. His hands worked over her back and shoulders, easing tight muscles.

When he shifted off her, she didn't move, merely lifting her heavy lids to watch as he pulled the covers over them both and settled in next to her. He propped his head on one hand, the other resting on the mattress between them. Mere inches separated them, and she knew they had been pressed together more closely in the escape pod, but this felt way more intimate.

There was one bed. That they had to share. And he was staring at her as if she was the most beautiful woman he had ever seen.

This reverent side of Domik was new.

He reached out a hand and pulled her toward him, tucking her against his chest and sliding one hand down her thigh to lift it over his hip.

She bit her lip, feeling exposed despite the oversized shirt she wore and the covers that shielded her from his view. But underneath the covers, she was aware of her lack of underwear. And yet she had never felt as safe as she did right now.

Heat pooled between her legs, and she flushed, ducking her chin to hide her face, hoping he didn't notice in the candlelit room.

"Clodagh?" His voice was dark and demanding and she looked up to meet his eyes. "What's wrong?"

"Nothing," she said, pulling her leg from his hip and tucking her arms around herself. He growled, clearly nonplussed by her response. "Honestly, nothing is wrong."

"I don't believe you," he said, pulling her against him, her backside nestled against his groin. Her back was against his chest. One of his arms thrown across her stomach to hold her against him. His hair slid over his shoulder to tickle against her neck.

She closed her eyes and, somehow, in the dark and quiet of the room, she found the courage to speak. "I find you attractive," she whispered, her face aflame at the admission.

"You find me attractive," he repeated.

"Yes."

His arm tightened against her stomach.

"I don't understand."

She rolled over to face him, lifting a hand to his face. "You are hot, Dom. Has nobody ever told you that?"

He shook his head slowly.

"Well, let me tell you. Your brooding, scowling presence does things to me."

"Things?" His eyebrows drew together in adorable confusion, and she grinned.

"Yes, things." She waggled her eyebrows suggestively, and he choked out a laugh. "And the whole bad ass warrior vibe you have going on? The hair, the muscles...?" She waved a hand in front of her face and huffed out a breath.

A slow smile spread over Domik's face, and he rolled away to stare at the ceiling.

This time it was CJ's turn to prop herself up on one hand. "I like you. I just wasn't sure how you felt about me."

His head turned, and he lifted a hand to her face, cupping her cheek. "You like me?"

She nodded, and he tugged her down toward him. Their lips brushed; his kiss surprisingly soft considering the sheer size of the man. CJ gasped, and he took advantage of the opportunity to explore her mouth. She lifted herself up and half over his chest, sliding her hands into his hair and deepening the kiss.

It could have been minutes or hours later, when he pulled away, breathing hard. "We should stop," he said, and her chest tightened at his words.

"Why?"

He brushed his thumb across her cheek. "It's been a long day. I don't want you to have any regrets. We probably went too far as it is," he said, a frown tugging at his lips as he pulled his hand away.

"Too far? It was just a kiss," she said, knowing it was a lie. This was not just a kiss. She doubted Domik did anything by halves. His next words confirmed her suspicion.

"I never do anything or say anything I don't mean, Clodagh. That was not just a kiss. Not to me." His eyes were warm as he met hers.

CJ felt something in her chest expand at his words. She smiled, reaching out to grasp his hand in hers. She ran her fingers over the ridges and valleys of his broad knuckles, tracing the many scars, some faint and others raised.

"I don't need you to do anything. To be anything... except you," he breathed.

"You know something?" She looked up at him, still holding his hand.

"Hmm?"

"That has to be the most words I've ever heard you say in one go." She winked and grinned.

He laughed. He actually threw his head back and laughed.

So there are two dimples.

She flopped down next to him on the bed, and reached down for the bedclothes that had fallen back at some stage, tugging them up over their bodies in the night's cool. He helped her, sliding an arm under her shoulders and tucking her against his chest.

He was so warm; her hand a contrast to his where it lay on his chest. He had such a broad chest she could hardly reach the far side. She pulled herself up onto one elbow and, propping her head in her hand, stared down at him.

He had one arm ticked under the pillow under his head, the muscles in his arms bulging in a way that she had seen before only on professional bodybuilders. Her mouth went dry as she drank in all the bronzed skin spread before her.

This was Domik. My Domik. Mine.

The vehemence of the thought startled her, and she stilled her hand, shooting a quick glance at him.

"What's wrong?" he asked.

Why did he have to know her so well? He always knew when she was upset, often before she had even registered that something was wrong herself. It was uncanny.

"How do you do that?"

"Do what?" He frowned, his face once more taking on the usual expression of stoicism she thought of as his resting Domik face.

"Know when I'm..." she trailed off, lost for the right words, and waved a hand absently.

He lifted a hand and smoothed it over her back. The gesture calmed her, and she pushed into his touch, like a cat being petted.

"You are easy to read, Clodagh."

She huffed out a breath. "Really? Then why do you always lose when we're playing chess?"

A slow smile tilted one side of his mouth before he replied. "Who says I'm playing to win?"

She smirked. "Those are fighting words. As soon as we get back to the Zataras, it's game on, big guy."

This time it was Domik's turn to lift on one elbow. The sheer mass of him looming over her stilled her breath. He was huge. More so lying down next to her, and yet she didn't feel one bit afraid. Quite the opposite. It was as if his presence, just like this, was enough to make her feel that everything was going to be OK.

He smiled down at her and dropped a kiss to her lips. His mouth was strong, his lips broad but gentle as he slicked his tongue against hers. She moaned, and he pulled away with a regretful smile.

"Get some sleep. Who knows what tomorrow will bring?" He dropped a kiss to her forehead.

She turned onto her side, tucking one hand under the pillow, and closing her eyes. Domik curled around her, dropping one arm over her waist, and pulling her close to nestle against his crotch—his still hard crotch—and nuzzle into her hair.

"Good night Dom," she whispered, closing her eyes.

Domik's hand, splayed against her stomach, moved backward and forward in a soothing motion that soon had CJ dropping into an exhausted, dreamless sleep.

CHAPTER THIRTEEN

Domik

As he dragged himself to wakefulness, Domik had the absurd thought that someone had removed his arm in the night. As his thoughts cleared, he realized he had been lying on it at a strange angle; the circulation having been cut off.

The light filtered through the gauzy curtains that covered the window, waking Domik. He kept still, listening in the early morning for any noises that didn't belong.

A bird called. The wind moved the leaves on the low, scrubby bushes outside, and he released a breath. All was well. He relaxed back onto the pillow, one arm behind his head, the other curled around CJ.

He looked down at her, watching as she stirred next to him, moving her hand where it rested on his chest, one of her legs thrown across his. Her breasts pushed against him as she breathed deeply, nuzzling into his side with an unintelligible mumble, before relaxing with a little snore.

Domik smiled, not attempting to hold back as he watched her.

Who was here to see, anyway?

Her face was relaxed in sleep, her lips slightly parted, the plump lower lip a little more red than the upper. He didn't need to wonder anymore what it would be like to kiss those lips.

He knew.

He had tasted pleasure beyond anything he had ever known, and now he held her in his arms. Trusting him to keep her safe.

It was a trust he would die before breaking.

He lifted his hand to smooth her hair, the short blond strands like silk under his fingers.

She opened her eyes at his touch, a small smile playing on her lips. "Morning," she croaked, grimacing at the sound of her voice. He smiled, and her eyes widened. "I could get used to this."

"Used to what?" he said, lifting an eyebrow.

"You. Smiling." She laughed.

Domik's chest tightened at her words. He gently pulled his arm free from underneath her, turning to sit on the side of the bed and bending to pick up the sweatpants from the floor.

"Dom?" Her uncertain voice had him stilling, one foot in the pants.

"Hmm?" He half turned toward her, not meeting her eyes.

"Are we... OK?" she asked, quietly. Then, in a rush, "I know we didn't say what this was, but I know this was a one-time thing." She laughed; the sound forced to Domik's ears.

"Sure," he said, standing and pulling on the pants with a quick jerk up and over his thighs.

What did you expect?

A small sigh and a rustle of sheets told him that CJ was getting up as well, the quiet snick of the bathroom door shutting behind her.

He sighed, dropping his head, and running his fingers through his hair, wanting to howl with frustration. As a child, he had studied with private tutors while children his own age played. As a teenager he had been at university, a gangling youth alongside adults.

No friends, and certainly no girlfriends.

Yes, he'd been advanced and had excelled academically, but socially, he had floundered.

It's a miracle you made it this far with Clodagh without her thinking you're the worst kind of weirdo.

He pulled on his boots, growling with frustration as he screwed his eyes up tight. He stood and thumped the wall with a growl, pulling the door open and stomping into the cool morning air.

The only way he had made friends had been if they wanted him for something, so he had learnt to make himself useful. It hadn't taken him long to realize that his supposed friends had just been using him to do their homework. So when he grew to his current build as a teenager, he'd downplayed his intellect, preferring his own company.

And that's the way he'd remained.

Until Clodagh had walked into his life.

The layer of grit on the concrete path crunched under his boots as he prowled toward the front of the building. Maybe he could make himself useful by finding more appropriate clothing to wear. He sighed, anger quickly dissipating as he reached the front office. He went past the reception desk and into the laundry room behind. This time, in the dawning light of day, he could see what he missed the night before in the dark. There were a series of baskets, all with folded clothing, ready to be returned to their owners.

Domik went to the first basket and upended it on the table in the middle of the workspace. Quickly sorting through the clothing, he pulled out what he hoped would be appropriate-sized pants for CJ. Then a shirt and a sweater and socks and underwear.

Finding clothing for himself was much harder, but he found a tee-shirt and a jacket, and some socks he hoped would fit. The rest he could make do with.

He was just stuffing the items into a backpack he had found under the bench when a distant noise had him freezing.

Once heard, you never forgot the sound of a Xakul ship.

His head whipped up to look in the direction of the room he had shared with CJ, as if he could see through the bricks and reassure himself she was safe.

Domik's hands shook as he forced himself to finish stuffing the clothes into the bag, before grabbing the handles in one hand and sliding from the room on silent feet.

I have to get back to her.

The noise of the ship was getting louder with every beat of his heart. He cursed his stupidity for leaving the pistol behind in the hotel room, and leaving wearing what? Sweatpants? Did he have a death wish? He knew better than that. He tilted his head, listening. The ship moved closer and closer, and now was almost directly overhead. Domik pressed himself against the wall of the motel, praying to gods he had long since given up believing in, as he moved as fast as he dared back to the room.

Please, just let her stay safe. Don't let her come out here.

As Domik looked up, the ship appeared, gleaming in the sunlight, the dark hull glinting every color and yet no color, like oil on water. But there was something different about this ship. A thought niggled at the back of his mind.

His hand was slicked with nervous sweat, and he growled, the door handle twisting in his grip. Yelling in frustration, he slammed his body against the door, falling into the room as the upper hinge tore from the frame. He fell to the floor, landing hard on his side.

"CJ!" he bellowed, scrambling to his hands and knees. He had barely gained his feet when he tripped over the fallen door, falling to his knees on the floor.

He struggled to hear anything over the sound of the Xakul ship overhead. He had to get to her.

He made his way to the bathroom, half crawling, half dragging himself with unsteady arms. The door was only partly closed, and he paused, breathing heavily.

If he pushed the door open and she wasn't there, his life would be over.

Lips thinned, he pushed gently, opening the door.

A soft whimper reached him, and he pulled himself into the room to see her curled into a ball inside the bathtub, her head buried in her hands, lying on her side.

Domik climbed into the tub, pulling her onto his lap. Her hands balled into fists and she flailed as he lifted her.

"Don't touch me! Let me go!" Her eyes were wild and

unfocused, sobs wracking her chest, tears pouring down her face.

Domik smoothed a hand over her hair, murmuring soothing noises as he held her gently in his arms.

"Dom?" she whispered.

"I'm here. You're safe."

She relaxed, the tension leaving her body. She drooped, limp in his arms, sighing and burrowing into his chest.

Domik glanced through the partially open door into the room. The door to the outside hung from its hinges, daylight streaming into the room. The noise from the Xakul ship quietened, the ship moving away.

They had been lucky.

He wasn't sure how long they sat there, his large form wrapped around hers, but she gradually settled and lifted her head from his chest.

"I was back there," she said, hazel eyes filled with tears.

Domik shifted, lifting her to her feet on the bathroom floor. "Where?"

"On Mars. The Xakul ships. You never forget that noise, you know?"

He nodded. "I know."

"They came so suddenly. I was in the clinic on the base, and there was a morgue—where they store dead bodies—so I climbed into one of the freezers and hid."

Domik stopped breathing. The thought of CJ hiding while those Xakul killed everyone around her.

She's stronger than anyone I've ever known.

"They left me there to die." She lifted her chin, her eyes pleading with him. "I thought you had done the same."

Domik's chest squeezed, and he dragged her into his arms. "Never."

She sobbed into his chest, arms gripping him tightly, her face pressed into him. She kept speaking, her words muffled, as if a dam had burst inside her and she couldn't help it. "The ships left, and the Xakul killed everyone left behind."

But they hadn't killed CJ. Domik knew the Xakul would track and kill anything once they had their sights set on them. They were unrivaled hunters. So how had she survived?

She lifted her head to look at him as she grimaced at her next words. "I hid in a freezer, but I wasn't alone. I masked my scent with a dead body."

Domik stared at her, eyes wide. She had lain in a freezer with a dead body. For how long?

"I was there for twelve hours before Laila found me. She had come in with the team she had been patrolling with. We were some of the few who survived."

Domik smoothed his hands down her arms and held her hands in both of his. "You are beyond strong."

She laughed, no joy in the sounds. "No. I'm not."

He shook his head, but she turned away, refusing to look at his face.

"Yes, you are. What you have overcome? Few could do what you have done."

She pulled her hands from his and wrapped them around herself, shaking her head. "No, Dom. That's just it. I have overcome nothing. I heard that ship and I couldn't move. The only thing I could do was sit in the bathtub and cry. What use am I? I'll just get people killed. It's a goddamned miracle you're still alive, being stuck with me."

She stepped backward until she couldn't go any further, the sink at her back. "Just leave me. You're better off without me. I'll just get you killed. Everyone is better off without me."

Domik frowned.

I can't leave you any more than I could cut off my arm. You are part of me, Clodagh. When you lack strength, you can have mine. Your sunshine lights my darkness. Without you, I am adrift in an ocean of loneliness.

He opened his mouth to speak, but seeing her stricken face staring at the floor, he thought better and stepped backward through the door into the bedroom.

I need to go get the clothes.

He opened the door to the outside and pulled up short.

About halfway across the carpark, was parked a pickup truck. The rumble of the engine must have been masked by the sound of the Xakul ship. Domik looked from the truck to the broken door of the hotel room, his palms sweaty as his fingers flexed for the plasma pistol that wasn't there.

How could I have forgotten it again?

He eyed the truck, not liking how close it was. In the dawn light, the windscreen was obscured in glare, hiding how many people were inside. He could see a human male behind the steering wheel, while another male was standing on the tray behind an enormous gun.

A gun that was pointed straight at Domik.

"Hands up!" The male in the back of the truck yelled at Domik.

He slowly raised his hands, backing up against the brick of the building, trying to get as far away from the room as possible.

The sound of the ship retreating slowly disappeared into the distance.

Why weren't the humans concerned about the ship?

It was difficult to tell the features of the man behind the wheel, , but the one in the back of the truck had a soft look about him. His clothes hung on him, as if they were for someone much larger, and his brown hair hung limp and greasy over his face.

The man pointed the gun at Domik, and as he did his shirtsleeve lifted, revealing a Taurean comm on his wrist.

What is he doing with a comm?

"Hey Tom, check out the size of this one!"

A soft click had him freezing. A third man emerged from the far side of the vehicle, a plasma rifle trained on him in a steady hand. "All right, big guy. Stay right where you are."

CHAPTER FOURTEEN

CJ

Gripping the sink, CJ took a deep breath. *I can do this.*
She forced her head up and met her own eyes in the mirror's reflection. The hazel was rimmed with red from where she had been crying.

She ran a shaky hand over her head, scrubbing at her scalp and running her fingers through the short strands.

The Xakul aren't here. I'm safe.

If only she believed it. The usual mantra had little effect when the sounds of a Xakul ship passing overhead had her curled up in the bathtub.

What would I do without Domik?

The question didn't bear answering. CJ had become so used to him always being nearby that when the Xakul ship had passed over and he hadn't been there, it had been as if she was right there on the base on Mars. Scrambling to find a hiding place in the medical center and squeezing into that freezer.

She turned on the tap and splashed cold water on her face, but froze at the voices from outside the room.

She whipped around to look out the bathroom door into the hotel room. Domik was standing by the door, his body outlined by the morning sun that was now shining brightly.

The male voices speaking English sounding strange to CJ after so many months of hearing Taurean translated or only female voices speaking her native tongue. The translator that was implanted in her head translated any languages into what she could understand, and Domik had one as well. They didn't actually speak the same language, though one day she would like to learn Taurean.

If you survive long enough, you mean.

She pushed the insidious thought aside.

But without a translator chip, nobody on Earth could understand Domik. And if they didn't know he was Taurean... well, he had to keep his mouth shut.

CJ watched as he stiffly lifted his hands up.

Oh god. What do I do?

She froze, one hand raised to her mouth as she watched Domik shift in the doorway, as if he was barring whoever was outside from entering.

Was he protecting her?

The voice came again.

"All right, big guy. Come out where I can see you."

Domik turned his head, his dark eyes intense as they met hers. He shook his head slowly and subtly tilted his head toward the bathroom.

Does he want me to hide?

CJ shook her head and Domik glared at her, lips pursed. He opened his mouth to speak and horror speared CJ. She shook her head furiously, holding a finger in front of her lips. He closed his mouth, but lifted a hand behind him to flick his fingers away from himself as if shooing her away.

She took a step into the room, and Domik's eyes widened.

"Come out. Now. Hands where I can see 'em." The voice was steady and almost bored sounding, which couldn't be good, but it was the fact that he was obviously armed that shot a shiver of terror down her spine.

CJ eased back into the bathroom, slowly closing the door. There was nowhere to hide. But there was a small window.

Can I fit through that?

As quietly as she could, she climbed onto the bathroom counter and eased the latch on the window and slowly opened it, her heart pounding loudly. A slight squeak of a hinge had her freezing, titling her head to listen for anyone coming toward her.

The only sounds were that of the man outside, muffled through the bathroom door.

What was he going to do to Domik?

She'd find out quickly if they caught her as well, so she pushed the thought aside. She stuck her head out the small window and, seeing nobody around, eased her shoulders through the small space.

If someone walks around the back of the building, I'm screwed.

She wiggled quickly through the space, the window frame scraping her skin. The drop to the ground wasn't far, but it was far from graceful, eliciting a groan as the impact pushed air from her lungs.

She quickly bounced to her feet and jogged around the side of the building, her bare feet smarting as the rocky ground bit into her soles. Reaching the edge of the building, she listened for voices and, hearing none, braved a glance around the corner of the building. A pot plant placed at a strategic angle blocked her from view.

She was at the far end of the motel, looking down at the long, rectangular building. The car park spread out in front of her, the only vehicle in it a large pickup truck. A man in the tray had a gun pointed at Domik, but dark tinted windows hid any other occupants from view.

Domik was standing in front of the broken door of the room they had been using, facing a second human man, who was keeping a safe distance. The man was wearing a plaid work shirt tucked into jeans, and cowboy boots were on his feet. Not the fancy type, the work type. And they were heavily scuffed.

But what really drew her attention was the plasma rifle in his hands.

A Taurean plasma rifle.

How did a human get one of those? Were these people working with the Taureans?

Her brows furrowed. That couldn't be. The only contact with Taureans had been through Space Force, the official military liaison with the alien race.

She watched as the man waved the barrel of the rifle at Domik, gesturing him toward the pickup truck. Domik glanced inside the motel room, obviously reluctant to leave, and the man took a step toward him.

CJ gasped, clutching her hands to her mouth, as the man fired the plasma rifle at Domik. Either he was a terrible shot, or he had meant to give a warning, going by the smell of ozone and the searing black mark on the ground at Domik's feet.

But Domik didn't flinch. His hands now lowered, he glared at the human.

Please don't do anything stupid.

The human man said something to Domik, but she was too far away to hear. The man turned his head and gestured at the truck. This time CJ caught the words he spoke. "Jock! Come watch him for a minute."

The other man hopped down from the tray of the pickup truck. "Sure thing, Tom." This man was shorter than his companion, still wearing the same style of shirts, jeans, and boots, but where the man with the plasma rifle made the outfit look like every day work clothes, this one looked like he was playing dress up with his older brother's clothing.

She watched as Domik's hands flexed at his side, fingers making fists and then releasing as the man from the tray, Jock, took the Taurean weapon from the other, Tom, who was obviously in charge. Tom walked toward the room.

"What are you so keen to hide, hmm?" He said as he approached the room.

Domik stepped in front of him, lifting an arm to bar Tom from entering the room.

"Want me to shoot him, Tom?" Jock called, his voice wavering with uncertainty.

"I don't know," he replied. Turning to Domik, he looked at the arm spread across the doorway. "Are you going to do something stupid? If we kill you, then we'll still find whatever is in that room that you're trying to hide."

CJ heard the growl that came from Domik, even being so far away, and her stomach flipped.

Just let him in.

She rubbed her arms, shifting from foot to foot as she

watched the interplay between the two men. Domik finally letting his arm down reluctantly, and Tom smiled triumphantly before entering the room.

Domik stared after him, his brows knitted.

I'm OK, big guy.

She drank him in, greedily memorizing every contour of his face.

It didn't take long before Tom emerged from the room. Domik schooled his face into his usual impassive expression, and she almost smiled.

How is he going to get out of this?

CJ held her breath as Tom held up something to Domik. Was that her boots?

"Not alone, are you?" He said, holding up the obviously too-small boots up for Domik to see.

Domik looked away, shrugging.

"I think that's why you didn't want me going into that room." The man turned toward Jock. "Do a check in the other rooms. Find her."

Shit!

CJ turned and bolted into the scrubby trees to hide.

Despite her panic, she remembered where they had left the bike and headed toward it, hoping to keep between her only way of escape and the men looking for her.

She paused, finding a place to hide behind a tree and a rock and, crouching down, watched as Jock walked around the building right past where she had been hiding.

He paused as he reached the open bathroom window and reached up, pushing it shut.

I forgot to shut the window. Oh no. She swallowed, suddenly feeling nauseous as she looked along the building. None of the other bathroom windows were open. *How stupid could I be?*

She shook her head. Jock continued more slowly, staring into the trees right near her. She held her breath, peering out from between the thick foliage that was hiding her. When he moved on, she could breathe once more.

CJ waited until he had rounded the far side of the building before moving closer. She had to see Domik. She had to know where he was.

She stuck to the trees, moving slowly as she peered into the carpark.

Her breath caught when she saw Domik.

He was on his knees, hands bound in front of him, and four men were standing around him in a circle with guns trained on him.

What had they done to him?

The one called Jock called out to the leader as he jogged toward the group. "Are we taking him back to the farm?"

"May as well. He's not talking, and we've got what we came for." The leader scratched himself as he spoke, then gestured to the back of the pickup truck, muttering something CJ couldn't catch.

She paled as she watched him yanked to his feet by his hands, and marched toward the back of the truck. He was pushed into the tray, his legs lifted by two of the men, who grunted with exertion as they lifted.

Why hasn't he resisted?

CJ chewed on her lip as she watched the rest of the men climb into the pickup truck. He didn't have long to break free.

She shifted from foot to foot.

Any second now. Come on, Domik.

Her heart pounded in her chest as she watched. The pickup truck started and then it began to slowly pull out of the carpark. She stared in disbelief. They were taking Domik away, and he had done nothing to escape.

Is he hurt?

She froze as she watched the pickup truck make its way to the carpark and then turn onto the main road.

Come on, Domik. Why aren't you trying to get away?

She turned toward the building, then back toward the direction of the bike, then the opposite direction where the pickup truck had gone.

What do I do?

A little niggle of a thought broke through.

He could have died coming back for me. I just sat there and did nothing, and he risked his life.

Domik had let himself be captured to keep her safe, to prevent her from being taken. He had bought her time to escape, had not resisted being tied up.

I have to help him.

But how? CJ squared her shoulders and, doing a quick check to make sure there was still nobody around, strode as rapidly toward the hotel as her bare feet would allow. She crossed the carpark and stepped over the broken door into the room that had felt so different last night.

What had been a haven, a place where she had bared herself to Domik, was now turned upside down. The mattress had been tossed off the bed frame, the meagre contents of the backpack Domik had stuffed full of clothes strewn around the room.

CJ rummaged through the debris, finding a pair of jeans and a sweatshirt that fit, and pulling on socks and her boots.

She grabbed the backpack and tossed in the largest shirt and pants she could find, remembering how Domik had been still clad only in sweatpants when he had been tossed into the back of the truck.

Don't think about it. Just get out of here and to the quad bike.

They must not have done a thorough search, because she found the plasma pistol. The reassuring weight of it in her hand bringing a sense of much needed calm. She grabbed Domik's thigh holster, quickly removing the leg strap to use as a belt, and tucking the pistol safely away.

Right. Time to rescue my man.

The backpack slung over one shoulder, CJ left the motel room and quickly jogged back to the where the bike had been stashed. She pulled the branches they had laid over the top to hide it and threw a leg over the seat. The bike started on the first try, and she breathed a sigh of relief.

It didn't last long.

Not knowing where they were heading would make finding Domik difficult.

I should have been ready to follow.

She shook herself and gritted her teeth. The past was just that, the past. Right now, nobody knew where Domik was, and she couldn't contact the Zataras for help. Hell, she didn't even know if anyone had survived. There was only one way Domik was going to escape, and that was if CJ helped him to do it.

She gripped the handlebars and turned the throttle, easing the bike onto the road after checking to make sure the coast was clear. There was no sign of the pickup truck.

Where would they have taken him?

She froze, remembering the men who had taken him

saying something about a farm. That excluded any of the houses in the small town. Feeling a little more hopeful, she opened the throttle and rode in the direction the pickup truck had gone.

I'll just check every farm I come across.

It didn't matter how long it took to find him; she would not give up. Not this time.

CHAPTER FIFTEEN

Domik

Everything hurt. His muscles were sore like nothing else, the skin on his wrists chafed raw from the tape used to bind his hands. His throat was dry, and he coughed as he tried to swallow. Cracking an eye open, he winced as pain lanced his head.

They had beaten him for resisting and not telling them what they wanted to know. He'd been half dazed when they had brought him here. Wherever here was.

All he'd been trying to do was protect CJ.

I should have kept her safe.

He groaned, dropping his head back down to the hard ground.

Where was he? Where was CJ?

He opened his eyes fully, wincing at the light that speared him. Blinking, he waited until his vision cleared.

The ground underneath him was cold and hard, made of the concrete humans seemed so fond of. There was a wooden door in front of him, heavy and stable, with solid hinges. The walls of the room were similarly heavy and wooden.

An animal enclosure? A...barn?

He lifted his head, turning onto his back to stare at the ceiling and noticing the small camera that was winking in the corner.

They would know he was awake soon, if they didn't already.

Domik forced himself to sit up, made difficult by the tape that bound his ankles and wrists. He lifted both hands to rub at his eyes, and push his hair out of his face. He shuffled backward until he was leaning against the rear wall, the door immediately in front of him.

This way, at least he would know who was coming at him.

He didn't have to wait long.

Footsteps sounded outside, getting louder as they approached him. A small window in the door opened, a face peering at him, before shutting and the door opening.

"Oh good. You're awake," the voice belonged to an older woman, a faded floral dress covered by a patched apron. "I have some food for you."

Domik nodded, staying seated and not moving.

She entered the room and placed a tray down near him, smiling and stepping away, watching expectantly.

Domik blinked up at her then, realizing she wouldn't leave until he had eaten something. He turned his head to look at the tray. There was a glass of water and a sandwich. He picked the glass up awkwardly in his bound hands, fumbling but managing to not drop it. He downed the water in big gulps, throat soothed by the liquid. Then, putting down the glass, he picked up the sandwich and ate.

It wouldn't have mattered what was on it, he was that hungry he would have eaten it, anyway. He groaned in appreciation at the first bite, swallowing and giving a nod of thanks to the woman. She crossed her arms across her ample bosom and nodded, as if satisfied with his efforts.

"A big, powerful man like you needs to eat," she said. "Don't know what kind of mess you are in ending up mixed up with that lot, and I suppose it's none of my business." Domik shrugged. She cast a look out the door before continuing quietly, "Do you even know who they are?" She tilted her head forward as if looking at him over the rim of an invisible pair of spectacles.

He shook his head, feigning a mouthful of sandwich to avoid speaking. If he could encourage her to keep speaking, maybe she would give him the information he needed to get out of here. To get back to CJ.

"They're the resistance," she said in a hushed tone, as if that answered everything.

He blinked at her, taking another mouthful of sandwich and chewing.

"You don't know who the resistance is?" she asked incredulously. "Have you been living under a rock?"

Domik shrugged again.

She huffed, rolling her eyes. "They think the alien threat is a hoax to control everyone. You've heard about that, right?"

He nodded.

"Right. Well, they think that other group of aliens doesn't exist and the Taurons—"

"Taureans," Domik corrected, his voice croaky.

"—whatever they're called—the resistance thinks they are just here to enslave us."

Domik choked on the mouthful he was chewing. His expression must have given away his feelings, as she laughed.

CJ is rubbing off on me if I can be read that easily.

"Exactly," the old lady said, and for a moment Domik thought she meant about CJ.

"I don't know what those boys think makes them such good slave material. Have you seen them? They're not exactly prime specimens." She shook her head. "You, on the other hand. You're as big as those, what did you say they were called? Taureans?"

Domik nodded.

Bigger than most, actually.

He finished the sandwich, and the woman bent down to pick up the plate and his glass. She smiled, straightening, before turning to leave. She stopped in the doorway, her voice a little louder. "I'm Georgina Jackson. This is my farm, or it was before those fools rolled in and insisted they were claiming it for the resistance. If my boys weren't in Space Force, they'd be here right now, and those fools wouldn't have dared mess with them." She scowled. "I'll be back later with more food."

Domik nodded and watched as she closed the door behind herself, opening the window and giving him a wink before walking away.

Maybe there's a way out of here after all.

Domik was no fool. He knew he could get out of this place, but he needed to know what he was facing before he tried. Who knew how long it would take to get out of here? Time was ticking. Every minute he was away from CJ, weighing on his mind.

He dozed off, head slumped forward, waking with a jerk as the door opened once more.

The person who stepped through wasn't the kindly Georgina. This time it was a skinny human—barely a man—who stepped hesitantly into the doorway. He was dressed as the others were, in a work shirt, jeans and boots, but a radio was strapped to his belt.

A radio.

That meant that there was a way to communicate. Perhaps there was a way to get in touch with the Zataras.

Domik shifted on the floor, rolling his shoulders as much as he could with his wrists bound.

The boy looked nervously over his shoulder, eyes pleading with whomever was still in the hallway. "Do I have to?"

Does he have to do what?

"Do it." A low growl came from outside the room.

The boy stepped into the room, eyes downcast and not meeting Domik's own. He was muttering under his breath, low words that Domik didn't recognize at first. A prayer. This boy was praying.

Why is he praying?

Domik lifted his hands in front of his face, as if afraid of the boy cowering on the floor. He was much bigger than this thin young man, but he pushed out a whimper.

I just have to get into the hallway. One step after the other.

The boy took a step closer, sliding his foot along the dusty floor.

It was almost night again, the fading light in the room casting shadows over the boy's face, making him appear even more gaunt.

"Oh, come on!" The voice in the hallway came again. "Do I have to do everything myself?" The speaker moved into the doorway, showing himself to be the man from the motel.

Tom. His name is Tom.

Tom stepped into the doorway, blocking the light from the hallway. His face was in shadow, his fingers flexing as he tilted his neck from side to side, cracking, before stepping into the room and shoving aside the boy who slumped onto the wall with a relieved sigh. "Get out of here," the man growled, and the boy fled.

Domik glanced from the doorway where the boy had gone back to his captor.

You've been through worse than this asshole can dish up.

Domik stayed slumped on the ground, looking up through half-lidded eyes. If they thought him weak and overcome, they might leave him alone.

No such luck.

The man smiled, his lips pulling back to show a missing tooth. The smile didn't reach his eyes. "So. Who are you, and what are you doing with this?" The man lifted the lifeless wrist comm from his pocket.

Domik's brows knitted in confusion.

"Don't think we don't know where this comes from. Those aliens think they can just come here and bribe us with toys like this and we'll do whatever they want? They leave us little 'presents' and we just go along with their enslavement of the human race?" Tom's face twisted into an ugly smile. "We'll die before that happens."

Is he insane?

The man stepped forward. "You're one of them, aren't

you? Those aliens. The ones spreading the lies about Earth being attacked. You're here to take us all away."

Domik blinked, not answering. Even if Domik could reply, even if this man could understand him, he was making no sense.

The man kept ranting, his voice loud in the small space as he stalked closer to Domik. "Are you going to tell me what you're doing here? Or do I have to find out from that woman of yours? I've got men are out there now, they'll find her." He grinned, a gap showing where he was missing a tooth.

So they hadn't found CJ...yet.

Domik fought to not show any emotion. Who knew how they would use it against him?

He's insane, and he is looking for CJ. I have to stop him.

He tensed, muscles primed as much as the bound hands and feet would allow, ready to spring. The man's words faded into noise.

One more step closer.

Domik willed the man to move closer, his foot lifting.

That's it. A little further and I'll have you.

Just as the man moved closer, the door opened, and he turned away.

Domik cursed under his breath as he watched the older woman, Georgina, carrying a tray into the room.

"Ah, Tom. They want you back at the house," she said with a smile, as if the ranting she must have been able to hear had not occurred.

Tom scowled at her, turning his back on Domik.

Domik smiled and prepared to launch himself at Tom, but Georgina shook her head, hiding the gesture with a brush of her hand to her hair.

"What do they want?" Tom asked, stepping toward the door, now out of Domik's range.

"How should I know? You're the boss, aren't you?" She moved toward Domik and placed the tray on the floor.

Tom left the room with a harrumph, leaving the door open as he did so.

Georgina stood still, waiting until the sounds of footsteps in the hallway had passed before turning to Domik.

"You don't have much time. There's a knife under the napkin. The door at the end of the hall opens out of view of the main house. There will be a truck parked near the shed on the other side of the main house. It's the best I can do."

Domik nodded, wishing he could express his thanks.

She straightened. "Not all humans are like those fools. Remember, that one helped you."

He nodded, watching as she turned and left the room, closing the door behind her.

The younger male's voice could be heard in the hallway as Georgina spoke with him, telling him he was also wanted at the main house.

Domik waited until the voices in the hallway had moved away, before sliding the knife out from underneath his leg. He grasped the handle in fingers that were almost numb from how tightly his hands had been bound. He fumbled, dropping it twice before wedging the handle against the wall and sawing through the plastic tie.

It was with considerable relief that it finally gave way, sending blood back into his hands with a rush that made his hands tingle painfully. He flexed his fingers, rotating his wrists and rubbing to bring the circulation back.

He had scraped his wrists while cutting free; the

serrations catching his skin and ripping it apart, but it was a wound he barely glanced at before picking up the knife from where it had fallen to the floor and, much more quickly this time, slicing through the tie binding his feet.

This one had been over the thick boots, not able to cut the blood flow to his feet, and he stood stretching out his limbs before approaching the door.

This had better not be a trap.

Domik closed his eyes, focusing his senses on the hallway outside. He couldn't hear anyone, but he couldn't believe nobody had been left to watch him.

Are they really that stupid?

He found it unlikely, but stranger things had happened. Like the Xakul passing over the motel and not sending soldiers to clear the place.

That was very out of character. Just like the ship they had used. It sounded like a Xakul ship, but there was something not quite right.

You can think about that later. Get out of here and find CJ.

His stomach clenched at the thought of the blond medic. He hoped, for the *resistance's* sake, that she wasn't harmed.

His lips thinned.

Don't think about it. Just get to her and get out.

The window into the cell was closed from the outside. He would just have to hope there was nobody standing silently outside. He lifted the handle to the door and opened it, easing it open a crack and peering into the hallway.

Empty. So far, so good.

He eased the door open further and, when no shouts came, peered out. Empty. The hallway was empty.

Domik quickly slid through the doorway, shutting it

closed behind him. He was standing in the middle of a long corridor, rooms like his own on one side, the other a solid windowless wall. He had been dazed when he had been brought here, carried by four human men, and he couldn't remember which way he needed to go.

But which way had Georgina's footsteps gone?

He turned to the right and continued slowly down the hallway, peering into the open doorways as he passed to ensure no one jumped out to surprise him.

He had begun to think he would get out of the building with no issues when a large figure stepped out of a side room a few feet in front of him, his back toward him.

Domik didn't think. He moved like lightning, grabbing the man from behind, one hand over his mouth and the other around his neck. He slid his arm deep under his chin, dragging him backward and into the, thankfully empty, room the man had stepped out of.

He was big, the tallest human Domik had ever seen, but still had nothing on Domik, who lifted his thrashing feet off the ground as the man pulled at his arm, desperately trying to free himself.

Domik squeezed his biceps tight, cutting off the circulation to the man's head and, eventually, he slumped.

Wasting no time, Domik laid him on the ground and, using the man's own belt, tied his hands together. He found a bandanna on a table in the room and gagged him.

Satisfied he wouldn't be able to make much noise when he woke, Domik left the room, shutting the door behind him.

He wiped his hands on his pants, smears of blood from the wounds on his wrists staining the gray fabric. The door at the end of the hallway was a solid wood. The barrier to him and the outside. Domik's luck had held so far, but it couldn't last forever. He had to be quick.

He turned the light off in the hallway, not wanting to draw more attention to himself than necessary, and left the building, sliding out into the cool desert night. Putting his back to the building, he skirted it until the main house that Georgina had mentioned came into view. The dark night offered many places for hiding, for both Domik and his captors, so he waited behind a stack of boxes, watching the stretch of open ground before him.

Where was CJ?

CHAPTER SIXTEEN

CJ

The ground was hard and cold where she lay on her stomach, watching the farmhouse where she was certain Domik was being held. For what felt like the hundredth time in the space of the last hour, she reached for the shotgun next to her.

Who would have thought there would be that many farms in the desert? She had almost lost count of how many places she had checked, all abandoned. But right when she was doubting herself, she spied the pickup truck that had taken Domik away. She had quickly hidden the bike and found a place to watch the farm.

That had been after midday, and she had spent the time since rejecting every plan to rescue Domik she came up with. It was now dusk; the sun was dipping beyond the horizon, and the temperature had dropped significantly. She hoped Domik was alive and not hurt.

She scanned the buildings in front of her again, watching

for any movement. The property was extensive, looking like there had been horses here once. There was a sprawling farmhouse, with a well looked after garden. Next to the house was a garage, the door shut, and the pickup truck parked in front of it.

Opposite the house, on the other side of the dirt drive, was a large barn. The solid wooden structure was where she suspected Domik was being held. She had seen an older woman carrying a tray of what looked like food across to the barn from the house, and then leave without it.

And now, as she lay on her stomach watching the barn, the leader—Tom, she recalled—emerged from the house, calling something over his shoulder to someone inside. A teenage boy hurried after him and even from this distance CJ could see he looked nervous.

What's going on?

A curtain twitched in the kitchen window, and the older woman's face appeared, watching the two walk toward the barn. It was hard to tell from how far away she was, but CJ could have sworn she scowled and shook her head. The curtain twitched again and within the space of less than a minute, the older woman appeared with another tray filled with food.

That was interesting.

When she reached the barn, she shifted the tray to one hip so she could free a fist to bang on the barn door. It opened outwards, and she disappeared inside.

CJ's lips twisted as she watched the barn. The minutes ticked by, achingly slowly, and then the leader and the teenager appeared again, the leader not as cocky this time.

CJ stood, making sure she was still hidden from view, and

picked up the shotgun. Just as she was about to make her way toward the barn, the older woman appeared. Instead of returning to the house, she made her way past it and toward a shed on the far side of the sprawling timber dwelling. The woman looked around furtively before dashing behind the shed and disappearing from view.

Not hesitating, CJ followed, making sure she was out of sight. She quickly crossed the distance to the shed, the lack of moonlight a blessing in hiding her from view.

She pressed against the side of the shed and risked a peek around the corner.

An old pickup truck was parked next to the shed, the front door open. CJ watched as the woman leaned inside and began rummaging around in the glove box.

If she had any hope of getting Domik away from here, she needed something a little better than a bike. Especially if he was injured. She winced, thinking about how she would get him to the military base that was still hours away if he couldn't walk. He would be completely impossible to move if he were unconscious.

CJ pushed the disturbing thoughts aside and crept toward the woman, who still had her back to her.

When she was close enough, she wrapped one arm around her neck and linked her arms, one hand over her mouth to smother her cry of surprise. CJ pulled her backward away from the car. The woman struggled, clutching at CJ's arms and kicking her feet.

"Where is he?" CJ demanded.

The woman's feet stopped kicking, and she relaxed a little.

"If I take my hand away and you scream, I'll knock you

out. Are we clear?" She was taking a massive risk, but getting Domik out without knowing more was going to be almost impossible. Especially since she did not know exactly how many men there were in the barn.

Or even if Domik was in the barn in the first place.

The woman nodded, and CJ eased her hand from her mouth.

"The big guy? The alien?" Her voice shook.

"Yes. Where is he? Is he hurt?" CJ risked taking her arms away from the woman's neck and turned her to see her face. She was older than CJ had expected and, for a second, she felt ashamed for having scared her. But then she hardened. One scared woman was worth Domik's safety.

"He's in the barn," she said, her eyes wide.

"And is he hurt?"

"No... or at least not badly."

CJ closed her eyes and breathed out. He was alive.

The woman tilted her head to one side. "He's your man, isn't he?" she asked.

CJ started. What? "Uh, kind of."

The woman smiled a knowing smile. "I'm Georgina," she said, offering her hand. "Those fools think those insect aliens are a hoax. Everyone else evacuated to shelters in the city, but they stayed behind."

"What about you?"

"I can't leave this place. It's been my home for forty years. It's all I have left apart from my boys. They're in Space Force, protecting us," she said. She smiled grimly and gestured upwards toward the stars before patting CJ on the shoulder. "Here." She handed CJ a set of keys. "Take the old truck and get out of here."

"Not without—"

"He's coming."

"What?"

"I gave him a knife. He'll be out in a few minutes, I'm sure." She turned around to the truck and picked up a bag that had been placed in the footwell, handing it to CJ. "There's food, water and a first aid kit in there. The truck is charged and should get you well away from here."

CJ took the bag and looked from it to Georgina, mouth open. "Thank you."

"You're welcome. Now keep an eye out for that man of yours and get out of here before that fool Tom realizes I've sent him on a wild goose chase." Georgina gave a chuckle.

"Are you sure you won't come with us?"

"Not a chance." She smiled and turned, walking away and disappearing around the corner of the building.

CJ stashed the bag behind the seats in the truck and stuffed the keys in her pocket. She jogged to the edge of the building and peered around it.

Come on, Domik.

From her vantage point, she could see the side of the barn, which was out of sight of the house. If Domik had escaped, he would need to make his way past the house where the men inside might see him. The sound of laughter drifted toward her from the house.

I can't believe these fools believe the Xakul are a myth!

She barely restrained a growl, instead turning to stare out into the night.

Domik, where are you?

A slight breeze pulled at her clothing, the cool night air making her shiver. An enormous shadow loomed on the far side of the barn, and CJ's heart skipped a beat as the shape materialized into the familiar outline of Domik.

She waved her hand back and forth to get his attention, and he lifted a hand in reply, holding his palm up toward her. Stay right there, he motioned.

Another peel of laughter from the house and the bang of the screen door reached her ears, and she looked from Domik to the house where Tom had stepped onto the porch, the screen door slamming behind him. She was frozen in horror as Domik stepped out into a pool of light that had spread from the house. If they looked now, they would catch him.

She frantically gestured for him to stop and go back, but he ignored her, dashing across the yard to reach her.

"Tom, I need to speak with you!" Georgina called from inside the house, and he turned, opening the screen door once more, his back to the yard.

I'm going to have a heart attack.

CJ held a hand to her mouth as she watched Domik sprint across the yard, faster than a man his size had any right to be, arriving at her side just as Tom turned around and walked down the steps and into the yard.

A moment sooner and Domik would have been seen.

"I don't know if that was stupid or brave," she whispered, her heart in her throat. "Come on." She clutched his hand in hers and dragged him around the shed, only letting go as they reached the old truck.

She opened the driver's side door carefully, wincing at the creek of the hinges, then slid onto the seat, shifting her hips so she could jam her fingers into her pocket to fish out the key. CJ reached up to flick the light off, not wanting to draw any attention to themselves.

Domik opened the passenger door and slid onto the seat next to her, turning as much as his large frame would allow. He reached out with shaky fingers to touch her arm, pulling back at the last second as if hesitant.

Domik? Hesitant? Since when?

"Let's get out of here first, OK?" She patted his arm in what she hoped was a friendly manner and, keeping the headlights off, started the truck, the electric engine almost silent in the still night.

Thank fuck it's not a gas-powered truck.

She stole a look at Domik, his bruised face in profile as he shifted on the seat beside her, his thick thigh pushing against hers on the bench seat. CJ sent a prayer of thanks to a god she had long stopped believing in, patting the steering wheel before easing off the handbrake. She shifted the truck into drive and eased it down the road.

With nervous glances in the rearview mirrors, the farm buildings gradually became smaller and smaller until, when the long driveway finally reached the main highway, CJ turned the truck toward their destination.

She hadn't dared to speak until they had passed through the gates and onto the main highway once more.

Feeling a weight shift, she cleared her throat, now able to ask what had been bugging her. "What did they do to you?" She asked, glancing from the darkened road to Domik and back. If his face looked this battered in the cab's dark, then they must have really worked him over. She winced in sympathy.

"Nothing that hasn't been done before." His voice was

rough, and he broke into a coughing fit, wincing as he held his side.

"Ribs?" she asked, knuckles tightening on the steering wheel. "There's water in the bag behind the seat."

If I had just five minutes with those cowardly assholes.

Shocked at the vehemence of her thoughts, she sat up straight in the seat and blinked.

Domik nodded, gasping for breath and holding his sides. "The medi-wand?"

"It's in my backpack, but it's not working. It ran out of charge." How she lamented the loss of what she had previously considered such an insignificant piece of kit. She had become so used to the advanced Taurean technology that something as life-changing as a medi-wand was now a tool that she would kill for.

Is it any wonder the humans so readily agreed to the alliance?

She sighed. It wasn't as simple as that. And since when had she started considering herself Taurean?

The night stretched out before them, the road long and empty. Soon they would be at the base and life would go back to... normal? She sighed. It wasn't as if this hadn't been coming.

"Can you sleep?" she asked Domik.

"I can try. I suppose you don't need me," he said, looking down at his hands that were piled in his lap.

What was that supposed to mean?

"What?" She glanced from Domik to the road and back.

Dom shook his head, still looking down. "I was meant to keep you safe, Clodagh." His eyes were stricken as they met hers.

"We were meant to keep each other safe." A note of steel entered her voice.

"I'm a genius, right?" Domik pressed on, shaking his head. "And a Taurean warrior, strong and dependable." He looked away, out the window. "And I wasn't even useful to you as that."

CJ's eyebrows shot up. "Dom, you let yourself be captured so I could escape. What else could you have done?"

He didn't answer, just shook his head and kept looking out the window. Surely he wasn't suggesting that she was so shallow that she only wanted him for his ability to act as a bodyguard?

He's tired and has just been through a lot, that's all. It means nothing.

But a little niggling thought pushed back.

Are you so sure he's that different? Everyone leaves you behind. What's to say he won't too?

She pushed the doubts aside, focusing on the dark road in front of them. "Get some sleep."

He sighed, turning away from her and laying his arm against the glass of the window and resting his head. He was quickly asleep, his face younger in repose. Long, dark lashes swept down over his cheeks, his mouth slightly open, chest rising and falling.

As the miles passed, CJ thought of all they had been through. The escape pod crashing, the Xakul attack, and Domik being captured and tortured by the resistance. And now their escape. She smiled, thinking about how she'd rescued him. CJ, the medic whose defining experience in battle had been to run and hide. And she had saved him. The biggest, scariest Taurean warrior of them all.

Would he have done the same for you?

Her smile dropped. If they had trapped her, she was certain he wouldn't have left her behind. Even so, the thought persisted.

She blinked, her eyelids getting heavy, and stifled a yawn. She would soon need to pull over if they didn't get to the base.

She mentally calculated how much time had passed and estimated how far they had traveled. No, they should make it to the base by dawn.

The Space Force military base.

The site of the first contact between Taureans and humans. She had read the reports about what had happened there, had heard from Oren and Amelia themselves.

Oren had crash-landed on Earth, and Amelia had helped him escape from capture on the base, both of them chased by a Xakul soldier who had fixated on them. Which was a typical behavior of the Xakul.

CJ shuddered. She should know. That's what they did on Mars. They had hunted down every single person they had seen. She was lucky she had stayed out of sight. It's the only reason she'd survived.

But she had watched the carnage on a tablet, trapped in the morgue freezer. It had been horrific.

So she had known intuitively what had happened on the Space Force base in the Nevada desert. Complete and utter carnage.

From one Xakul soldier.

So, why did that ship at the motel not send soldiers down to take them all out? Not just her and Domik, but the resistance as well?

It makes little sense.

The Xakul presence and the Taurean technology that was scattered around was an added complication. Someone from Taurus had to be working with the resistance, and she bet it was the Taurean Purists.

It was the only solution that made sense.

The Purists were a hateful group who wanted no mixing of Taureans and humans... or any other species. They felt Taurus was being polluted by contact with humans, and that helping them fight off the Xakul was akin to helping vermin.

Thankfully, the Taurean Purists were a minority, but there had to be someone powerful behind them, because how else had they delivered Taurean military technology to Earth?

She was certain she was right, but the real question was, why?

CJ pondered as she drove, the truck devouring the miles as they made their way toward the Space Force base outside Las Vegas. As the dawn light broke over the horizon, she crested a hill and in the valley before them; the base was spread out.

They must have an alternate source of power generation, as there were floodlights on the gate. And, as CJ turned down the long road toward it, she could see a glow in the distance around which she knew the buildings on the base were located.

Domik woke, blinking sleepily as he sat up and stretched, tilting his head from one side to the other. "Almost there?"

CJ nodded. "Yes."

Domik twisted in his seat to reach for the pack CJ had thrown behind them, pulling his plasma pistol free and running checks to ensure it was working.

"Do you think that's a good idea?" CJ asked. "We're not in uniform and you're huge... and armed."

Domik shot her a smirk. An actual smirk, and her insides melted. She had been trying to get him to smile for months, and now that he was, it felt like sunshine blasting her after an arctic winter. Like scalding hot water when you expect it to be cold. CJ was wondering if she would survive emotionally if Domik really showered her with attention.

The truck bounced along the road, CJ seeming to find every pothole. Domik grunted as she hit a particularly big one.

"Sorry," she said.

As the gate loomed ahead, CJ began slowing the truck. She lifted a hand to shield her eyes against the lights as they approached.

Domik's hand reached across to press on her arm. "Slower."

She nodded, pressing the brake pedal and slowing to a crawl.

An automated message blasted from a loudspeaker. CJ winced at the noise. "You are approaching a Space Force installation. Stop your vehicle at the barrier and raise your hands. Do not attempt any sudden movement."

CJ shot a glance at Domik, who nodded, his face a solemn mask as he gazed toward the light. She moved forward until she reached a boom gate, where she stopped the truck, putting it into park and raising her hands. Domik did the same, but not before resting the pistol between his knees. Out of sight of the guards, but not out of reach.

The thought was reassuring to CJ.

How did I get to trusting an alien more than my own people?

A guard approached; his own gun held at the ready. He paused, gun raised to his shoulder, masked face cast in shadow from the floodlight behind him. "Slowly get out of the vehicle, hands raised where I can see them!" He shouted, his accented voice belying his southern origins.

CJ swallowed and glanced at Domik, her heart pounding in her chest. "Dom?"

He turned toward her, dark eyes solemn as they met hers. "I'm right here, Clodagh. I'm not leaving you. Not again."

She nodded, finding the strength to open the door of the truck.

Will they believe us?

She took a deep breath and stepped onto the tarmac with her hands raised.

Only one way to find out.

CHAPTER SEVENTEEN

Domik

Domik watched as CJ got out of the truck, her hands raised as she stepped to one side.

The guard, clad in the black Space Force uniform of combat pants and jacket, and heavy boots, turned to look at Domik through the window. "You too! Get out of the truck!" His voice was hard and Domik hoped this wouldn't turn to violence.

I don't want CJ to get hurt.

Domik opened the door and slid out of the truck, lifting his hands he unfurled to his full height. The guard tilted his head back to look up at him, taking a step backward.

"Who the fuck are you?" the guard asked, as the drumming of rapid footsteps sounded on the road.

Another half dozen armed men emerged from the light, identically clad, standing at a distance with their guns raised. Domik noted that none of them was trained on CJ, only on him.

Good.

CJ took a hesitant step toward Domik then, when the armed guards didn't react, another until she had closed the small gap to stand partly in front of him. He growled a warning, and she pushed a hand backward as if to hold him back.

It was laughable that she thought she could protect him.

Didn't she already do that?

He swallowed, hating that she would need to be the one to put herself in danger yet again. That he couldn't be understood.

I am going to learn the language of her people. This is untenable.

"We're here to see General Russell," she said, and the first guard laughed.

Domik took a step forward, stopped only by CJ's small hand on his chest.

The guard laughed again. "Sure. And I'm the Queen of Sheba. Nice try lovely."

CJ bristled. "My name is Sergeant Clodagh Jones. I am a veteran of the Mars attacks and am assigned to the Taurean Starship Zataras. Our shuttle was damaged in the defense of Earth and our escape pod crashed. We have made our way here to speak urgently with General Russell." She crossed her arms over her chest and glared at the guard. "What we have to say will interest him. You don't want to get in our way."

"Is that a threat, girl? Don't you see what you're dealing with?" He laughed, turning to gesture at the soldiers to either side, and Domik had never wanted to choke someone more badly in his life.

CJ smiled, but it didn't reach her eyes, continuing as if the stupid human hadn't spoken. "Did I forget to introduce my friend? How rude of me. Domik, why don't you tell them who you are?" She looked up at him and winked.

Domik growled, taking a step forward, ignoring the rifles that tracked him.

Good. If these idiots shoot someone, it won't be her.

Domik opened his mouth and let all the frustration of the past few days come out. He knew that none of the humans would have translation chips, except for CJ, so they wouldn't understand the words he spoke. So he let loose in an uncharacteristic display of frustration. "You are all a bunch of fools. The Xakul are going to tear you all apart because of your ignorance, and I won't be sad to see that happen. At least there will be more targets for those insect bastards."

He turned his head and met CJ's wide eyes. "It wasn't the shuttle escape, or the crash, or being captured that was the worst thing to happen to me in the past few days. It wasn't even the beating I took." He reached a hand to brush away a smudge of dirt on her cheek, uncaring that the soldiers were watching him. "It was being separated from you."

CJ's mouth dropped open as she stared up at him. He broke away to step in front of her and face the Space Force troops once more.

"I am Specialist Domik Vo'Ress of the Taurean military, stationed on the Starship Zataras. And you will all die if you don't listen to her."

The leader, who had been stunned into silence, shook himself. "What did he say?" He said to CJ.

"Oh," she said, smirking as she peered around Domik's side. "Couldn't you understand Taurean? No translation chip then, hmm?"

159

The man swallowed. "He was just speaking shit. Get back in the truck and drive away. You're not getting on—"

"Stand down, corporal." A hard voice came from behind the line of Space Force troops, a tall figure emerging from the flood of light. "Did you say you were Sergeant Clodagh Jones? The survivor from Mars?"

CJ blinked, trying to focus. The figure stepping in line with the troops and finally becoming clear. A woman, eating an apple. CJ raised an eyebrow; she wasn't fooled by the casual attitude. The way the Space Force marines just moved out of her way told CJ this woman was the person who had to be convinced to let them on the base.

CJ tilted her head, looking the other woman up and down. "Yes, that is what I said."

The woman took a step closer, Domik growling in a low rumble. He didn't like this.

"And he said his name is Domik Vo'Ress, is that right?" She ignored Domik's growl and walked closer, stopping just out of striking distance.

Smart woman.

"You have a translator." CJ moved out from behind Domik, resting a hand on his forearm.

He had to trust that she knew what she was doing. He wasn't one for politics or talking. Just get in, do the job, get out. That was his motto. The dancing around and word play? That was his brother Oren's forte, not his.

And he felt very much out of his depth here. And outgunned. It was a distinctly uncomfortable feeling.

Domik watched as the two women eyed each other, CJ's discomfort obvious.

"I'm Major Sarah Adams. You're famous, you know." The

woman grinned, stepping forward to grip CJ by the shoulders.

"Ah, no. I'm not, ma'am," CJ replied.

"No, no. You really are. All the survivors are." She rattled off a list of names, ticking them off on her fingers. With each name said, CJ's face became more pale until Domik held up a hand to make her stop.

"Oh, sorry. That was insensitive of me." She grimaced. "You said you wanted to see General Russell, is that right?"

CJ nodded. "Yes, ma'am. We have an urgent message to give him."

She turned, linking her arm in CJ's leading her toward the gate. "Let's get you two to the General then," she said, gesturing for the marines to fall back and let them pass. "Leave the truck, we'll take care of it. Come with me."

Domik retrieved the plasma pistol and their pack from the truck before following CJ and Major Adams to a military truck nearby. They climbed in, and began moving through the barriers at the gate, bouncing along the long road toward the center of the base.

The major chatted animatedly as they drove, Domik tuning her voice out, instead watching as the dawn light spilled over the road, the streetlights winking out as they passed. After a few minutes, they approached a cluster of buildings, CJ pointing to them.

"That's the hospital where your brother was, and where Amelia worked," she said, giving him a soft smile.

Those few days of not knowing what had happened to Oren were some of the most harrowing of his life. His brother had a job that kept him offline for days, or sometimes weeks, at a time. That was true. But when he had crash-landed on Earth, it had been a different matter entirely.

Shaking his head, Domik watched as they passed the hospital. The looming brick building cast in an orange glow in the morning light.

"Here we are," she said, slowing the truck and turning down a side road and toward a series of low buildings. She pulled the truck to a stop in front of the central building and turned off the engine. They climbed out and moved up a set of steps that led to glass double doors with gold lettering embossed on them.

Domik looked at CJ with an eyebrow raised.

"Space Force Central Command, Earth Operations," she read for him.

He appreciated she understood his need to not feel on the back foot. He needed to know what was going on.

The major walked to the door in front of them, waving her badge at the guard, who opened the door for them to enter. They entered a foyer with a single metal desk bolted to the floor, behind which a marine stood, looking up as they approached.

"Good morning, ma'am," the young human male said, saluting. "Please sign your guests in."

Domik bristled at the layers of bureaucracy preventing him from talking with the human general. It felt like every second was ticking past, wasting time that they could use to communicate with the Taureans.

A doorway to the right was flanked by two guards, heavily armed with Taurean plasma weapons. The general must be in an office behind that door somewhere. Domik turned, approaching the guards.

"Tell them to let me through," he said over his shoulder, not breaking stride as he marched toward them.

"Stop!" they shouted in unison, lifting their rifles.

Fools. Don't they know how to use those?

Domik reached them in two strides, batting the barrels of the rifles out of the way, before grabbing them and tossing the weapons across the room.

He turned and held a hand out for CJ, who shrugged apologetically at the other woman and ran across the room to put her hand in his.

Domik smiled and, tugging her after him, pushed through the double doors and into the hallway beyond.

Despite the hour of the day, there was a lot going on. In front of them was a glass wall that overlooked an open office, a door in its middle. There were lots of humans in uniform working in front of view screens at desks, and talking.

Domik rapped on the glass and a balding man with more fancy braid on his uniform than Domik had ever seen, turned with an annoyed look that quickly dissolved as he looked up and up to meet Domik's eyes. The man scrambled backward, tripping over his chair and sprawling on the ground. The rest of the room's occupants turned to look as Domik rapped on the glass again.

CJ opened the door and yelled into the room. "Where's General Russell?"

The man who had sprawled on the floor lifted a shaking hand to point to a door on the far side of the room.

Of course, the man would have a private office. Not for him to be out amongst the workers.

CJ and Domik strode across the room, not paying any attention to the hushed whispers that followed them.

When he reached the door they had been shown, he turned a questioning look to CJ, who nodded.

"That's his office, going by the sign on the door," she confirmed.

Domik pushed down the handle and stepped into the room, CJ following to close the door behind her.

This was a large room, a desk set before a wall of windows that overlooked a lush garden. Domik didn't want to think about how much water a garden like that would use in a desert.

What a waste.

He shook his head, taking in the rest of the room. At the desk sat a harried, familiar looking human male. The man had lifted his head as CJ and Domik entered the room, scowling at their intrusion as he pushed to his feet. He gestured toward the door. "Who let you in here?"

CJ walked into the room, ignoring the general's question. Domik followed to stand at her side.

"Sir, my name is Sergeant Clodagh Jones. I am stationed on the Starship Zataras. You must listen to us," her voice pleaded as she spoke.

The general glared at them as they approached his desk. "I don't have to do anything."

"But, sir—"

"I know who you are, Sergeant. And it's because of who you *both* are that I will tolerate this intrusion."

Domik growled and stepped closer to the desk. The general took an involuntary step backward as Domik approached, but, to his credit, lifted his chin and stared him straight in the eyes. "What do you want?"

CJ gently tugged Domik backward. "Sir, we need to get a

message to the Starship Zataras, if it survived the attack, or Taurus High Command."

"Didn't you hear?" The general looked between them before walking around the desk to lean against it, arms crossed over his chest. "The Taurean fleet arrived hours ago. The Zataras held the Xakul off for quite a while, and took considerable damage, but it's still up there. Fighting."

CJ and Domik shared a relieved look.

"And what of the Xakul?" Domik asked.

"There have been skirmishes when they've broken through the Taurean defenses, but it hasn't been the all-out assault we had feared." The general raised an eyebrow. "Is this why you broke into my office?"

"No, sir," CJ said. "We have news about an alliance between some humans and a Taurean terrorist group."

The general ran a hand over his face. "Go on."

If there was one thing that being held captive had given him, it was time to think. So he told CJ and the general his conclusions. "The human resistance believe the Xakul are a hoax, yes?"

CJ and the general both nodded.

"But they acknowledge Taureans are real," he said with a roll of his eyes. "The Taurean Purists don't want a human alliance with Taurus. They want the Taurean genetic code to remain pure." He emphasized the last word with a distasteful twist of his mouth. "It's in the best interests of the Purists for humans to either be wiped out or to break the alliance with Taurus."

The general rubbed his chin thoughtfully. "So you think these Purists are interfering, but they don't really care what the outcome is of the Xakul attack, as long as Earth suffers."

Domik nodded. "Exactly."

"So, how are they interfering?"

"By providing arms to the resistance and encouraging them to cause trouble on Earth. And by attacking the Taurean fleet to prevent their arrival here in time to stop the Xakul attack - they were the reason the fleet was delayed and almost didn't make it in time."

The general pressed his lips together and reached for the comm button on his desk. "You're right. This needs to go to Taurus High Command."

CJ reached for Domik's hand and gave it a squeeze, which he returned. A warm glow spread through his chest. Their job was done.

There was no reason to stick together now, was there?

As the thought sent a chill through him, he looked out of the expanse of glass to see a swarm of Xakul ships appear, heading directly toward them.

"Down! We're under attack!" Domik yelled, grabbing CJ and throwing her to the floor, covering her with his body.

CHAPTER EIGHTEEN

CJ

The first blast rocked the building, shattering glass and making CJ's ears ring. She struggled for breath, gasping. Domik's bulk covered her where she lay on the floor, a big hand cradling her head close to his chest.

She squeezed her eyes shut, burying her face into his chest and holding her breath as glass shards rained down on them. Domik grunted as something slammed into him, but still he clung to her.

Please don't let him be hurt!

Her ears rang from the blast, her hearing dulled. She felt, more than heard, the rain of chunks of brick and the creak of metal from the roof above them.

After a few heartbeats, Domik eased himself off her with a groan, flopping to one side and wheezing.

"Dom?" CJ sat up, running her hands over him to check for injuries. "Let me see your back." He was lying on his side, so she stepped around him, almost losing her footing on a piece of brick in her haste.

His back was a bloody mess of torn skin. There was no way he hadn't broken something.

The sound of creaking metal filtered through her dull hearing, and she turned to see what had been the glassed wall teeter before falling slowly toward them.

CJ cowered, throwing herself over Domik's prone form as the frame crashed to the floor.

We will not die! I didn't go through all this to die by being squashed in a falling building.

CJ gritted her teeth as the floor shook around her once more, blasting dust around them. She blinked, clearing her vision.

She was still lying over the prone form of Domik when she lifted her head. The sight that met her had her laughing almost hysterically.

The frame had missed them by mere inches. If they had been a little further to the right, they would have been crushed.

Don't think about that. Just move.

CJ lifted herself off Domik and shook his shoulder. "Dom? We have to go. I can't carry you."

He groaned; one eye cracking open. "Leave me."

"No." She scowled at him. As if she would ever leave this great lump of a man. Alien. Whatever. It didn't matter what he was. He was hers. And she was never letting him go.

"I can't—"

She cut him off with a growl. "If you want me to live, you had better get your ass out of here. Because I'm staying right with you, whether you like it or not."

Domik blinked at her, before breaking into a coughing fit and wincing. It was obvious he was in a lot of pain, and she wished she had something to help him. She hated to make him move, but it wasn't safe.

She helped ease Domik to his hands and knees, blood running down his arms like a river. She winced, gripping him around the waist and taking as much of his weight as she could to help him to a kneeling position.

He braced his hands on his knee and panted, his deep eyes locked on hers.

"You can do this, Dom. Do it for me." She hated manipulating him like this, hated seeing this strong, proud warrior look so vulnerable.

He was strong for me when I needed it. I can be strong for him. He needs me, and I won't let him down.

He nodded and braced himself as he rose to his feet, CJ sliding an arm around his waist to steady him. She staggered slightly under his weight, and they almost crashed to the debris-strewn ground, but he caught himself with one hand against the remaining wall, hissing with pain.

CJ took one last look around what had been the pristine office of the general. The doorway they had entered was a pile of rubble, the window-filled wall now a gaping hole. CJ nodded toward the garden beyond.

"That way," she said, and they staggered over the piles of bricks and glass.

As they stepped through the opening and into the garden, a wind picked up and, looking overhead, the underbody lights of a Taurean shuttle lit them up.

Domik grunted and staggered onto the lawn, falling to his knees, taking CJ with him. She ignored the noise of the shuttle overhead, not even noticing the Taurean warriors who descended until one tried to pull her away from Domik.

"No!" she cried, fighting against their hold, feet kicking uselessly against the ground as she was lifted bodily away. Her arms were useless against the armor-clad warrior who held her, his words lost as she watched another warrior press something to Domik's neck and then he collapsed, face first, onto the lawn.

"Domik!" she screamed his name over and over until the press of cool metal on her neck brought darkness.

———

W hen she woke, it was to stare at khaki green canvas. She tried to speak, but just croaked.

"Here," a familiar voice said, "drink this."

The familiar face of Dr Amelia O'Malley swam into CJ's vision, and she lifted her head, aided by Amelia's hand behind her neck, and took a long pull of cool water.

"How long?" CJ croaked, lifting a bandage-clad hand to her face.

"About an hour," Amelia said.

"When did you get here? The others?" CJ took another drink of the water, letting her head fall back to the pillow.

"Not in time to stop the Xakul attack that you saw, but we chased them off." She grinned. "The others are fine. They all made it back to the Zataras before the EMP."

CJ closed her eyes, letting the relief wash over her. When she opened them again, she looked past Amelia, her white coat and bright red hair in contrast to the darkness in the canvas tent.

A field hospital, then.

"The hospital?" CJ asked.

Amelia's lips pressed into a thin line. "Destroyed in the Xakul attack."

CJ reached out and grasped the doctor's hand. "I'm so sorry."

Amelia took a shaky breath. "I would have been in that building, but Oren wouldn't let me out of his sight." She looked over her shoulder to where the Taurean intelligence officer could be seen standing near the entrance to the medical tent. "I'd be dead if it wasn't for him." She smiled softly, then turned back to give CJ a soft smile.

"Where's Dom?"

Amelia lifted an eyebrow. "It's Dom now, is it?"

CJ flushed, but held the doctor's gaze. "Yes. Where is he?"

"He's over there." She gestured across to the other side of the tent.

CJ pushed up to a sitting position and swung her legs over the side of the stretcher. Her head swam, but she waved the doctor off with a dismissive hand as she braced her hands on her knees and pushed herself to standing.

She staggered between rows of stretchers with injured Space Force marines and Taurean warriors being treated for minor injuries. Domik was lying on his front on a stretcher and turned his head as she approached.

"Dom," she said, her eyes widening at the broad expanse of his back now stripped of his shirt. The skin had been torn apart in places, blood streaking across his bronzed skin.

A nervous-looking human medic was holding a pair of forceps and, as CJ watched, reached down to grab a shard of glass with shaking hands and pull it out of Domik's back. The medic wiped sweat from his forehead with the back of his hand and prepared to repeat the task, but stopped when Domik shifted on the stretcher.

"Clodagh," Domik said, his voice hoarse. He reached for her hand and squeezed it before closing his eyes tightly.

"I'll take it from here," CJ told the medic as she placed a proprietary hand on the only undamaged part of Domik's back she could see.

Nobody is going to touch him except me.

The medic paused, the forceps he'd been using in one hand as he looked from CJ to Amelia, who nodded. "Go on, there's plenty more who need your help." He shot a relieved look at CJ and put the forceps down before moving on to another patient.

CJ squatted down next to the stretched, making sure she was level with Domik's head. "I'm going to take care of you, Dom." She brushed his hair away from his face and he closed his eyes, tension leeching from his muscles. She dropped a kiss to his brow and stepped away to where a sink had been placed and quickly scrubbed her hands.

"Will you be ok?" Amelia asked from where she had stopped next to CJ, resting a hand on her friend's shoulder. Her blue eyes were intent as she examined CJ's face.

"Yes," CJ said, surprised to find that it was the truth. "I'll be fine."

Amelia smiled and patted CJ on the back before heading back through the stretchers on her rounds.

CJ gathered the equipment she needed and pulled up a stool next to Domik's stretcher and began working on his back. She worked in silence, his hand dangling toward the floor, resting on her ankle in a possessive claim.

She looked up as Oren pulled a stool up on the other side of Domik's stretcher. She smiled softly at him, and Oren nodded in greeting, his brow pressed into a slight frown as he watched CJ work.

Minutes turned into an hour, and when she was finally finished, she stood and stretched. Domik lifted his head, his eyes glazed with the painkiller he'd been given.

She grabbed one of the few medi-wands that this small field tent had available and waved it over his back. She shook her head as she watched the muscle and skin knit before her eyes, leaving faint silver scars behind that crisscrossed his back.

When she was done, she turned off the medi-wand and gently cleaned all traces of dirt and blood away from his skin, smoothing her hand over his back. He watched her from half-lidded eyes before closing them and, finally, drifting to sleep.

"Is he asleep?" Oren asked.

"Yes." CJ pulled a folded blanket from a nearby empty stretcher and draped it over Domik, a small smile playing on her lips.

"You care for him." It wasn't a question, but a statement.

More than you will ever know.

CJ said nothing, just smiled slightly as she smoothed the hair back from Domik's face, tucking it behind his ear. His long dark lashes swept over his cheeks; his face relaxed in sleep.

Oren said something, and CJ realized she hadn't caught his words. "Sorry?" She looked up.

"I said he cares for you as well."

CJ straightened, sitting upright and ticking her hands into her lap. She knew Domik cared about her. He'd showed as

173

much over the past few days. But in the way Oren was suggesting?

She wasn't entirely convinced he hadn't kept a lookout for her out of some misguided sense of responsibility. He'd said, more than once, that everyone else on the team had someone.

Laila and Zac had each other, as did Krystal and T'arq. Oren and Amelia had... something, though they both played their cards close to their chests.

But CJ? She had nobody.

Had he been looking out for her just because she was the sole singleton?

CJ rubbed her chest and grimaced at the thought.

"Has he told you how he feels?"

CJ shook her head slowly. "No. He's been very kind to me, though."

Oren barked out a laugh. "Kind? Domik?"

"Yes. Why wouldn't he be kind?" CJ scowled up at the older brother of the man she had come to—what, exactly? Did she love him?

Oren smiled, and CJ's heart lurched as she saw those same dimples appear on his cheeks. The two brothers were so very different in so many ways. But perhaps that was because Domik rarely smiled?

"Domik doesn't get close to anyone. Have you ever asked him why?" Not waiting for a reply, he slapped his thighs and stood. "Now I know my big little brother will be fine, I have work to do. Those Xakul won't hold off for much longer."

CJ's head snapped up.

Oren nodded, the smile falling from his face. "They'll be back, and when they return, we need to be ready."

It was the reminder of the mysterious Xakul ship they had seen at the motel that had CJ gasping.

"Oren, we saw a Xakul ship."

He sat up straight, all signs of the caring brother gone. He was now the Taurean intelligence officer, eyes focused intently on her. "Where? When?"

"It was the first night after we crashed in the pod."

"That makes no sense," he said, rubbing his jaw.

"I know. We were in a motel, and it just flew over. But the weirdest thing was the resistance fighters who grabbed Domik—" She swallowed, feeling sick as she remembered those harrowing hours being separated from him and not knowing if he was dead or alive.

"Go on." Oren encouraged, his voice gentle.

"The resistance fighters acted like they expected the Xakul fighter to be there. They weren't bothered by it, and it didn't attack them."

"Tell me exactly what happened."

So she went over everything that had happened since the pod crash-landed. Well, maybe not quite everything. There were some secrets that she didn't want to spill.

Oren rested his elbows on his knees as she spoke. His head dropped forward as he listened. Occasionally, he asked her to clarify something, but mostly he just nodded in silence.

"I need to take this to my superiors in intelligence," he said when she was done.

CJ stood. "What can I do?"

"Stay with him until he wakes. Make yourself useful with the wounded. When he comes to, we'll need him doing what he does best."

"And what's that?" CJ couldn't help but ask.

Oren smiled ferally. "Killing Xakul." Then he turned and left the tent.

She stood and, with a last glance to make sure the Domik was comfortable, headed to where Amelia was treating a patient with a bandaged arm.

As the morning progressed, the tent heated, and soon CJ was stripped to her tank top. She lost count of how many patients she tended. She had learnt the more serious injuries had been evacuated by air; the Taureans having been able to mobilize some shuttles and send help to the Space Force bases that had been attacked by the Xakul.

She would check on Domik between patients, making sure he was still comfortable and resting. She knew he would need a fair amount of sleep even after the use of the medi-wand, particularly because his wounds had been so many.

It was toward midday when the wail of a klaxon started, sending a chill through her. She turned to find Domik pushing off the stretcher, and she raced toward him.

"You can't!" she cried; eyes wide.

"I have to," he said, sitting on the edge of the stretcher. He lifted a hand to her cheek, cupping it and stoking his thumb gently over her skin.

CJ swallowed and nodded. "Promise you'll come back to me?"

Domik stood bare-chested, his head touching the roof of the tent, but he didn't answer her. Choking back a sob, she watched him leave without looking back.

CHAPTER NINETEEN

Domik

Leaving CJ was the hardest thing that Domik had ever done. He knew it was necessary, but still. It hurt.

And he had a score to settle. Stepping out of the medical tent, he watched as troops, both human and Taurean, ran every which way. A truck bowled past, horn blaring as it tried to get through a throng of people.

Domik turned on the spot. The medical tent was toward one side of a small tent city that had been erected near the destroyed Space Force headquarters building. In the distance, the smoking remains of the hospital he remembered from his last visit could be seen.

That explains the field hospital.

Domik snagged the arm of a passing Taurean. "Tell me, where is field command?" The man pointed toward a nondescript tent with a solitary human marine standing guard and, with a nod of thanks, Domik headed toward it.

He didn't pause as he entered, just pushed past the guard,

who stepped back at Domik's sheer size and the growl that split the air, and opened the flap. He stepped into a room filled with a large table, overhead fluorescent lights throwing a bright white light in the darkened interior.

Three familiar faces looked up as Domik entered, and he smiled. "Zac. Brother. T'arq," he said in greeting as the three Taureans moved to greet him, clasping forearms in the traditional warriors' greeting.

"Let's get you some armor," T'arq said, moving toward a trunk and tossing Domik some dark gray Taurean uniform pants and shirt.

He stripped right there, pulling off his boots and the sweatpants he still wore, which were now beyond filthy and now an unrecognizable shade of brown. He paid no attention to the other occupants in the tent, only looking up when he was fully dressed in Taurean armor once more. When he approached the table where the three warriors were scanning various maps, they looked up.

"I'm glad to see you are alive," Domik said, nodding at all three.

"Pretty hard to kill, we are." T'arq laughed.

Zac nodded, a grim set to his jaw. "Oren tells us you saw a Xakul ship."

Domik nodded, turning to his brother. "Did Clodagh tell you that?"

"Yes, she also said the resistance seemed to expect them."

Domik scrubbed a hand over his face. "I've been thinking about that. They were expecting a ship, that much was obvious. And the ship sounded like a Xakul ship. But when it flew over, it didn't quite look like any Xakul ship I'd ever seen."

The three Taureans glanced worriedly at each other.

"And we never saw a Xakul soldier."

Oren lifted an eyebrow, and the two brothers spoke in unison. "The Taurean Purists."

A collective gasp was heard as those around the table realized the implications of this.

"What would they want with us?"

Domik turned to see General Russell step forward, his head bandaged and his arm in a sling. One side of his face was swollen and bruised, and blood marred his torn uniform.

"It's not what they want with you. It's what they were hoping the resistance will do."

"And that is?"

"To start a fight between humans and Taureans, so the Xakul will have less resistance to take Earth."

The general sat heavily in a chair, staring sightlessly. "So we get wiped out."

Domik nodded. "Yes."

He laughed; the sound crazed. "Too bad for them. We aren't easy to kill, either."

You haven't seen Xakul soldiers in battle.

But Domik kept his mouth shut and let the general be surrounded by his staff.

The wail of the klaxon cut off suddenly, the lack of noise strange.

"Here they come." A human voice cried.

Domik threw a look at the other three Taurean warriors and, as one, they strode from the tent.

The look that Oren shot toward the medical tent wasn't lost on Domik.

My brother, we are both caught in the web of a human.

"Heavy weapons?" he asked, grabbing Oren's arm. His brother dragged his eyes away from the medical tent and gave himself a shake.

"This way," he said, turning and striding purposefully away.

The four warriors strode toward the edge of the tents where a Taurean stealth ship sat.

"Hello, baby," T'arq crooned as he walked toward the vessel. A hatch on the top popped open and a curly brown head popped out.

"Hey, Domik!" Krystal called down. "Glad to see you're not dead!"

Domik lifted a hand in greeting, as T'arq jogged toward the ship and pulled himself up and into the cockpit with effortless movements.

Zac pointed toward the edge of the airfield where a circular structure made of concrete could be seen. "Your gun is waiting for you." He clapped Domik on the back and strode away.

Oren joined Domik as they jogged toward the concrete structure. It didn't have a roof and, as they approached, he realized why.

There was a small opening in the wall, though which they squeezed, before dropping about two meters to get to the bottom of a pit. The pit itself was about ten meters across, the walls thick concrete that rose another three meters above the ground. The walls were reinforced with concrete and in the center was something that made Domik smile.

"Oh, I hate it when you do that," Oren grumbled.

"What?"

"Smile like that. It's creepy."

Domik laughed and turned to run his hands over the giant gun that filled most of the pit. It was anchored in the middle on a circular disk, designed to spin a full 360 degrees. The gun's turret was currently pointing slightly up, and the height and angle of the walls meant it had been hidden as they approached.

The structure was of Domik's own design, one he had developed as part of a special project for the Taurean military.

Most knew of him as a weapons specialist, but he was really *The* Weapons Specialist for the Taurean military. He just liked to conduct his testing in the field.

Domik pulled himself up a short ladder to sit on the small seat behind the controls. He waved at Oren to join him, his brother taking the jump seat slightly to one side and behind Oren.

This gun was operated by two warriors: one as a spotter, and the other as the main controller.

Oren was familiar with this weapon, having helped Domik develop it in his early years at the Taurean military academy.

"Let's get those insect bastards," Oren snarled, grabbing the helmet from the hook and pulling it on.

Domik did the same, pressing the button for the heads-up display that came across one eye, similar to that which T'arq would have as the pilot of the stealth ship.

He hit the sequence of buttons to fire up the gun and tested it with a few short spins on the disc, and elevating it so they could fire over the top of the concrete wall. The view from up here gave him a sight across the desert plain where the base was situated. The midday sun beat down, hot and bright, and the comm channel connected to their helmets lit up with alerts of incoming Xakul fighters.

"Oren?" Domik shouted over the noise of the gun and the comm channel chatter.

"Coming in at a bearing of 015," came the reply.

Domik swung the gun around to face almost due north, knowing better than to rely solely on his eyesight to spot the fighters, but still straining to see, anyway.

Please be safe.

He forced himself to focus on operating the gun and, as the first enemy fighter shot toward them, instinct took over as all hell broke loose.

Seconds felt like minutes, and minutes felt like they had passed so quickly it made no difference. The first fighter was in range before he realized and was shot down, the body of the aircraft exploding into debris overhead.

And then it continued. One after another, Oren called the fighters and Domik shot them down. Wave after wave of fighters falling from the sky. T'arq and Krystal did their fair share with the stealth shuttle, too.

One after another, they shot at the Xakul fighters, which seemed to come at them in an unending wave. Theirs wasn't the only gun of this type on the base. There were another half dozen scattered around the perimeter.

The first to be destroyed by a Xakul ship exploded in a fireball that shot tens of meters into the sky. The shock wave shook the walls of their bunker and Domik gritted his teeth and kept firing.

The Xakul soon changed their tactics and began flying at the guns from directly into the sun, making it difficult to see.

One after another, the big guns were destroyed until it was just Domik and Oren left. And still they fired.

I made her a promise. And I will not break it.

Domik let loose a harrowing howl that shook the surrounding air, gripping the controls tightly as his hands flew faster than they had before.

I am coming for you, Clodagh. Life is nothing without you.

Again and again he fired, until one made it past all his shots, flying like a demon this ship kept coming, the black shape menacing as Domik gritted his teeth and bellowed his rage as he fired shot after shot.

"Two hundred meters!" Oren shouted from behind him.

Domik fired, over and over again.

"One hundred!"

A shot clipped the wing of the enemy ship, but it corrected and still came at them.

"Fifty!"

And then it was there. Almost on top of them. Domik threw everything the gun had at the fighter as it flew toward them, letting loose a battle cry like nothing he had ever screamed before.

A shot finally struck home, tearing the fighter in two and sending the debris flying. But half of the shuttle kept coming for them, toppling end over end as it wrought a path of destruction towards them.

"Brace for impact!" Domik shouted, showing his hands up in a futile attempt to protect himself from impact.

CHAPTER TWENTY

CJ

The sounds of the battle raged around them as CJ worked alongside Amelia as wounded fighters were brought in and then sent back out to battle.

"When are the reinforcements coming?" She asked for what seemed like the hundredth time.

"As soon as they can." Came the answer.

And so she put her head down and did what she could to help, and tried not to think about what was happening. How was Domik?

I've been such a fool.

She shook herself. It didn't matter what had come before. Nothing mattered except him. Nothing.

How could I be so blind? I love him.

She paused in bandaging an arm, the medi-wand-long since run out of charge, and pressed a hand to her sternum as she fought back a sob.

You are strong. You are brave. You can do this.

She took a deep breath and continued. Looking after Taureans and humans alike. One Taurean came in with a piece of metal the size of CJ's fist embedded in his shoulder. His uniform was torn and bloody and, as CJ cut it from him, she distracted him by getting him to talk. His face was pale, his eyes the same piercing green as Zac's.

"Where were you when this happened?" she asked.

"On the gun. You know the big ones?" he said, grimacing as he moved to let her get to the back of his shirt.

"I haven't seen them." She scowled as she looked at the metal. It was in too deep for her to remove, it could be preventing massive blood loss. "Amelia?" she called across the bed to where the red-haired doctor was working on another patient. When she looked up, CJ gestured to the shrapnel. "I'll need you for this one."

"Give me a second to finish up here."

CJ readied the equipment Amelia would need and continued speaking with her patient. "Tell me about the guns."

"They're a Vo'Ress design, built into the ground. Best ones we've ever had," he said with a proud smile.

"Vo'Ress? Not Domik Vo'Ress?" She asked, eyebrows shooting up in surprise.

"Yes, he's the designer. A genius, really. Every modification he's made to our weapons has made them safer to use, and more effective." He turned his head as Amelia approached, greeting her with a grimace as he shifted on the bed.

Domik designed weapons?

She knew he was a specialist, and he'd alluded to making modifications to Taurean weaponry. But she didn't realize he had been the designer as well.

What was he doing on a small combat team?

It was confusing. She acted on autopilot, passing Amelia what she asked for. The patient was sedated, and the shrapnel quickly removed, the mobile medi-wand quickly knitting torn muscles back together.

"He's lucky," Amelia said as she watched the mobile machine work.

"Hmm?" CJ turned to her friend. "I'm sorry, I was distracted."

"Worried about Domik?" Amelia gave her a small smile and patted CJ on the shoulder. "I'm sure he'll be fine."

But will he? If he would be anywhere, it would be on one of his own guns, surely?

CJ's eyes drifted over her patient.

He could have been Domik.

She sat next to the stretcher on a stool and watched as the machine worked, marveling not for the first time at the advanced Taurean technology that made what would have been a complex medical procedure into something minor.

When the machine beeped to show it was finished, CJ moved it to the next patient that needed it. And so on for hours, until the battle suddenly went silent.

Domik. I have to get to him. I have to see if he's OK.

She lifted her head, looking across the room to meet Amelia's eyes.

"Go," her friend mouthed, nodding toward the door.

CJ didn't need to be told twice and ran, dodging around

stretchers and medics, dashing to the door and racing outside.

It was chaos. There were people rushing everywhere. A truck was on its side, smoke coming from inside. She stood, mouth agape, as she looked around at the carnage. How the medical tent had been spared, she did not know. A large hole was in a nearby tent, a group of marines spraying fire suppressant foam on a blaze that was threatening to overwhelm it.

A honking horn had CJ leap back to prevent being run over by an ambulance, the vehicle screeching to a stop next to her, and the driver and passenger jumping out to open the back door.

"Get out of the way!" One of them shouted, and CJ dashed away.

Which way had Domik gone?

He would have been operating one of the heavy guns on the perimeter of the camp. That was his area of expertise. But those guns - of his own design, she now knew - were scattered around the edge of the base, and it would take far too long to find him on her own.

The familiar noise of a rapidly approaching Xakul fighter had her ducking, hands over her head. She looked up to see the fighter being chased by two Taurean vessels, one a stealth ship. Neither was bothering to use the cloak now, preferring to be visible to the ground-based guns.

A stream of rapid plasma fire shot from one of the Taurean ships and the Xakul fighter lurched off course, tumbling in a spiral toward the distant hills.

Then another Xakul ship flew overhead, to be taken out by a volley of shots from the ground. A gigantic explosion rose from somewhere behind CJ, and she turned to see a fireball rise rapidly into the sky, followed by a cloud of smoke.

The wind picked up, blowing smoke and dust, and she covered her mouth with her hand.

One of the Taurean shuttles circled overhead, before slowing and starting to descend near the edge of the camp.

CJ took off at a sprint. That was a stealth ship, like what T'arq flew, and she bet that would be where she would find one of the team to tell her about Domik.

Please be all right. Please.

Her booted feet pounded on the hard-packed dirt, her arms pumping. The afternoon sun hit her in the eyes as she ran, and she lifted a hand to shield her face. She watched as the shuttle turned and disappeared behind a row of tents and CJ dashed between them, tripping over a box and going sprawling.

She ignored hands that offered to help, blind to anything but her need to see Domik.

To know that he was all right.

To know.

No matter what happened to him, she needed to know.

And so she ran. Faster than she had ever run before. She slid around a corner, booted feet skidding on the gravel, arms wheeling as she fought to keep her balance.

Her tank top was slicked with sweat, her breath coming hard as the stealth ship finally came into view, settling down on the landing pad. She came to a stop, holding her breath as she watched the stealth ship power down and the hatch pop open.

She pressed a hand to her chest as she gasped for breath, watching as a curly brown head popped out. CJ sagged to her knees.

At least one thing is going right today.

"CJ?" The voice came down from above. "Quick, lift me down, T'arq."

And then there were soft footfalls as her friend ran toward her.

"CJ? What's wrong?" Krystal skidded to a stop next to her, laying a hand on her back.

CJ looked up, tears flooding her eyes. "Domik." The single word was all she could say before

CJ raced toward the stealth ship, arriving just as Krystal's booted feet hit the ground. She threw her arms around the small woman who had become one of her closest friends. Krystal smiled and hugged her back.

"Is it over?" CJ asked, pulling back to look over the shorter woman. Krystal looked a little worse for wear, soot darkening her cheeks and staining her purple flight suit. She had unzipped the front of it to reveal her tank top underneath, which was soaked with sweat.

"Yes, it's over." Krystal rubbed a hand over her face, her exhaustion apparent. She turned as T'arq climbed down from the cockpit and landed lightly on the ground behind her. He slid his arm over her shoulders, pulling her back against him.

"It's good to see you're OK, CJ," he said, a small smile lifting one side of his mouth.

"Likewise," she said, punching him lightly on the arm. "Not that there was any doubt the fleet's cockiest flyboy would come out shining."

He laughed. "Not with such precious cargo."

CJ's chest clenched, and she swallowed, all humor lost.

"Where's Domik?"

T'arq turned and pointed across the expanse of bare ground toward a gun position, his smile fading as he surveyed the scene before him. CJ gasped and fell to her knees, blood pounding in her ears as she took in the destruction.

She had seen the concrete bunkers on their way in, standing solid against the barren desert. It had seemed like nothing could crumble them.

But now?

No. No, it can't be. He can't be buried under all that.

She gasped, her blood rushing in her ears, blocking the words that T'arq said. She pushed Krystal's concerned hands away and staggered to her feet, rushing across the field toward the pile of rubble that had once been the gun bunker.

One side of the circular structure remained; the rest was blown to pieces. The gun's turret stuck directly up toward the sky, but was twisted at an odd angle. The body of a Xakul ship was embedded on one side of the bunker, a wing dangling over the ground like a bizarre parody of a beach umbrella.

How anyone could have survived that she could not imagine. But she had to see for herself. She wouldn't rest until she had seen Domik. She had to know.

CJ ran as fast as she could, feet pounding against the hard dirt, her breath coming in pants. Sweat poured down her face, running into her eyes. She rubbed at her forehead, wiping away the sweat, some making it into her eyes to make them sting.

And still she ran.

She wasn't that far away when T'arq's shouts finally broke through her panic.

"CJ! Stop!"

She turned her head to glance briefly back at him, lips pressed into a determined line. She turned her head back just in time to see a dark figure loom in front of her before she ran smack into a solid wall of muscle.

She went down in a tangle of limbs, letting loose a shriek of fright.

Strong arms picked her up, cradling her against a muscled chest. CJ wiped the dust from her face and looked up into familiar black eyes.

"Domik?" she gasped, a smile splitting her face. She grasped his face in her hands, pressing kisses over every bit of him she could reach. "I thought you were dead," she cried, tears rolling down her cheeks as she finally pulled back from her assault.

"It takes a little more than that to kill me." He smiled, both dimples appearing in his cheeks, and CJ's heart thundered in her chest.

"Is it really over?" she asked.

"For now," he said, smoothing a hand over her hair and pulling her against his chest. "I'm glad you are unhurt."

CJ laughed, happier than she had been for a long time.

"All right, you two," T'arq panted as he arrived. "That's enough standing around."

Domik kept hold of CJ as he turned and started towards the center of the base.

"Hey! I can walk, you know," she protested, pushing against his chest halfheartedly. Domik lifted an eyebrow, and she sighed. "All right, you can carry me. As long as you're not hurt."

He grunted, shifting her in his arms before striding toward the tents.

The look T'arq and Krystal shot each other was not lost on CJ, who blushed but lifted her chin and met their stares with defiance. Let them think what they wanted.

"What about Oren?" CJ asked quietly, knowing if anything had happened to his brother, Domik would be reluctant to talk about it.

"He's at the medical tent."

CJ stiffened. "He's hurt?"

Domik looked down at her, brows creased. "He's fine. He went to find Amelia."

CJ sagged, banging her head against Domik's chest. "Don't scare me like that."

He pulled her closer to his chest and dropped a kiss on the top of her head. "I apologize."

She snuggled closer, breathing in the scent she associated with Domik. A slight hint of spice, the ozone smell of plasma, grease and sweat. It wasn't unpleasant.

It didn't take Domik long to eat the distance with long strides, and they were back at the medical tent. He placed her gently on her feet. "You'll be needed here."

She nodded, turning toward the entry to the tent through which she could see wounded on stretchers, before stopping and turning to Domik.

"Dom?" she asked, looking up at him with wide eyes.

"Yes?"

She licked her lips, finding the courage to speak words she had never uttered before. "Don't leave me again."

He pulled her against his chest, wrapping his arms around her and sighing. "I need to meet the rest of the team for the debrief, but I'll be back."

She looked up at him. "Do you promise?"

"I promise."

CHAPTER TWENTY-ONE

Domik

He watched as CJ entered the medical tent. Feeling like he was letting something precious slip through his fingers.

Not for long. Stick to the plan.

Domik turned and headed toward the command tent.

It had taken being separated from her to realize what he needed to do. And he would let nothing get in his way.

I've been such a fool.

He shook his head, a scowl giving him a fierce expression so that anyone in his way avoided meeting his eyes, and quickly stepped to one side.

In the past, that would have made Domik happy. Having people move away from him meant they wouldn't engage in conversation with him. They wouldn't get to know him and be able to hurt him.

Over time, the habits of his childhood had become so ingrained that he had become to think that he was unlikeable. That people, when they didn't want to use him for his brain or his size, really were just scared of him, women especially.

Until she had seen right through me.

A warmth filled his chest as he thought of all the times she had questioned him. Pushed back. Refused to let his superficial answers to her questions go.

Bit by bit, she had eroded the walls he had built to protect his heart, so slowly that he hadn't realized it was happening until he felt exposed. Raw.

And it had begun with one smile.

He had spent his life maintaining barriers, making sure people stayed away, kept their distance.

Then he had walked onto that sports court back on the space station base orbiting Taurus those many months ago and he'd taken one look at her and everything had changed.

He didn't want her to be afraid of him, or to keep her away.

Instead, he stuck close, learnt that she had her own demons, and wanted to help her defeat them.

Now he was ready to begin anew, and he wanted her by his side, but only if she wanted to go willingly.

So he had a proposal.

Before he spoke to CJ—Clodagh—he needed to see Zac.

He approached the command tent and, pushing aside the flap of canvas, stepped inside. The room had lost its frantic tone, many of the Space Force marines nowhere to be seen. The view screens were black, except for a section on one side of the tent where a Taurean was directing personnel of both species, coordinating the movement of wounded to orbiting starships for treatment.

Domik looked around the room, spying Zac standing to one side talking with the human general. Domik approached and stood a short distance away, patiently waiting his turn to speak with his commander.

Not for much longer.

Zac turned and gave Domik a warm smile, the scars on the left side of his face pulling slightly as he did so. He nodded to the general, who turned and moved away, before sliding his arm around Domik's shoulders.

"It's good to see you, my friend," Zac said, and Domik realized he was right. Zac was a friend.

It was good to have friends again.

Again? Had he ever had friends before?

Domik shook away the thought.

"Thank you." He gave a small smile in return.

Zac gestured for them to sit, pushing away papers and tablets to one side of the table. "What can I do for you, Domik?"

Domik settled his hands on his knees and stared at the warrior who was a friend and confidant. "I have a request."

Zac waved a hand for him to continue.

"I was recently contacted by Taurus High Command. They want me based on Taurus. In a weapons research and development position."

Domik watched as his commander and friend nodded.

"And you want to accept." It wasn't a question.

"Yes."

Zac leaned back in his chair, one foot lifting to rest on his knee, arms crossed. He leveled an assessing gaze at the big weapons specialist. "Are you sure about this? Won't you miss the action?"

Domik huffed out a laugh, getting a raised eyebrow from Zac in response.

"I am sure."

"Have you spoken to CJ about this?" Zac asked.

Domik sat up straight in the chair, eyes narrowing. "Why would I need to do that?"

"Domik, you don't need to hide with me. I've known for months how you feel about her."

He had? What else had Zac noticed?

A hand landed on Domik's shoulder, and he turned to look at his brother Oren. "We've all known how you feel about her." He gave his shoulder a shake before pulling up a chair and dropping into it.

"What?" Domik looked between Zac and Oren, suppressing a groan when T'arq appeared to pull up a crate and perch on it with his legs stretched out in front of him.

"Will you teach me how to play chess, CJ?" T'arq mocked, pulling a face.

Domik glared at him, balling his hands into fists.

"That's enough," Zac said, before turning to Domik. "He has a point, though. You have genius level intellect. We all know you can thrash us at any game of tactics. Because you have. Repeatedly."

Oren laughed. "But her? You never win a game. Ever."

Domik crossed his arms over his chest, glaring at them all.

Bastards. Why won't they just shut the hell up?

"You will not be able to glare your way out of this one, Domik," Zac smiled, leaning forward and pushing a flask toward him. "Here."

Domik took the flask and uncapped it, taking a swig of the fiery spirits and grimacing at the taste.

"That's the stuff," said T'arq, holding a hand out for the flask which Domik happily surrendered.

"That's awful," he gasped.

"Yep," said T'arq, wiping his mouth. "But it sure takes your mind off what you need to do next."

Domik must have looked confused.

"Tell her you love her."

Domik held out a hand for the flask, and the three warriors who were his closest friends in the world laughed.

———

I t was a short while later, showered and dressed in a clean uniform, that Domik approached the medical tent. He pushed a hand through his hair, stopping when he touched the tightly braided strands.

For the first time in days, he felt clean. Truly clean. He had shaved the stubble from his face, cleaned what felt like a thousand layers of dirt and grime from his skin and even filed back his fingernails and applied a cologne that T'arq had offered to him.

He figured it couldn't hurt, but now, catching a sniff of himself, he wasn't so sure.

I smell like a bouquet was dunked in a bottle of whiskey.

Grimacing, he took a breath and pushed on, ducking inside the medical tent.

He blinked, his eyes adjusting to the changed light inside, as he looked around for CJ.

Most of the stretchers were now empty, neatly folded

blankets on the end and a single clean, white pillow stacked on top. They were arranged in neat rows, the orderly appearance at odds with the chaos of earlier in the day.

Domik strode across the tent, toward the center where a group of human and Taurean medical staff were talking. As he approached, their conversation broke off, and they turned to stare.

But he had eyes only for the blonde woman who had her back to him. She was the last to turn, looking over her shoulder and smiling broadly when she spied him.

His heart lurched in his chest, and if there was any doubt in his mind, it was quelled.

I love you.

His whole being screamed with the emotion and it was a wonder to him that everyone around didn't fall over at the extreme feelings that shot through him.

CJ strode toward him, and a huge smile lit his face as he met her in the middle of the tent. He ignored the onlookers and dropped to one knee in front of her, taking her hand in his. Her eyes widened in shock as she lifted her other hand to cover her mouth.

"Dom?" she whispered, clutching his hand tightly. "What are you doing?"

He smiled slightly, their heads almost the same height as he kneeled before her. "Clodagh, I have something I need to tell you."

"Oh." Her face paled as her hand dropped away to clutch at his. "What's wrong?"

Domik swallowed and steeled himself before saying, "I lied to you, Clodagh."

She blinked. "What?"

"I lied to you," he repeated. He looked down at their joined hands before continuing. "Or I may as well have. I didn't actually lie to your face, but I let you believe something that wasn't true."

She tilted his head to one side, lifting a finger to her lips in mock deep thought. "Did you kick a puppy?"

"What? No. Of course not." He shook his head.

She lifted an eyebrow. "Did you hurt someone on purpose? Apart from all those Xakul, I mean?"

He shook his head. "No."

"Then what could be so bad?"

He squeezed her hand gently. "I never had to stay on the Zataras."

"Huh?" She shook her head and blinked rapidly, as if that would make sense of his words.

"I was offered a position on Taurus months ago. As chief weapons designer for the Taurean fleet."

"Why do you think this means that you lied to me?"

"I never told you the truth about why I stayed."

She smiled.

Maybe everything would be all right?

She leaned forward to throw her arms around his neck and plant a quick kiss on his mouth. "You could never lie to me."

"But—"

"No buts. I always know when you try to hide the truth. There's not a dishonest bone in your body, Domik Vo'Ress."

Domik's chest felt like it would explode with happiness. "But I lied about chess," he protested.

"And I knew you were letting me win," she said, pulling

back from him slightly, her shoulders shaking as she tried not to laugh.

"You did?"

"Of course I did!"

"Then why didn't you say something?"

"For the same reason you let me win, I imagine. I wanted an excuse to spend time with you, and I was too afraid to say anything in case you didn't feel the same way." Her eyes were soft as she smiled at him.

He gathered her to him, kissing her with all the pent up passion of the months they had spent dancing around each other. He slid his tongue along the seam to her lips, feeling a surge of joy as she moaned and her lips opened under his.

He bit back a groan as he nibbled on her bottom lip, teasing and licking as she became pliant in his arms. When he pulled his head away, she gave a little mewl of protest and he smiled against her closed lips, watching as her dazed eyes opened.

She smiled up at him, both oblivious to everyone around them, until a small cheer rose from the assembled medics.

Amelia stepped forward. "Congratulations, you two. We were wondering if you'd ever get the guts up to admit how you felt to each other." She smiled. "Why don't you go see Oren outside? He has a surprise for you both."

"What is it?" CJ asked.

"I do not know," Domik replied, standing and taking CJ's hand in his.

Amelia just smiled conspiratorially and gave a shrug. "You'll have to wait and see."

Domik turned to CJ. "Shall we?"

She nodded. "Let's see what this surprise is."

CHAPTER TWENTY-TWO

CJ

She wasn't a fan of surprises, but with Domik's hand in hers, she figured she could face whatever Oren had to tell them.

They stepped outside of the medical tent, Domik spotting his brother first. He pointed at a black pickup truck that was stopped not far away, Oren leaning against the side, his feet crossed at the ankles and his arms over his chest.

As they approached, he pushed off the truck and lifted a hand in greeting. "I thought you two might like somewhere private to go for a few days. Sorry we can't fly you there, but they lost too many shuttles in the attack, and they can't spare one for hours. I figured you'd want to go earlier than that."

CJ's eyes widened as she glanced between the two brothers.

"Thank you," Domik said, before guiding her up into the passenger seat of the large truck and shutting the door. He stood for a few moments talking with his brother, before taking an envelope and pocketing it.

He climbed in next to her and started the engine.

"Do you know how to drive?" She asked.

"How hard can it be?" He said, staring at the steering wheel.

"Oh no, no no no. Get out. I'm driving." She unbuckled her seatbelt and went to open the door, but a bark of laughter stopped her.

Was Domik actually laughing?

She turned to glare at him. He rested an elbow on the steering wheel and faced her.

"I can drive. Trust me." He smiled, and she grumbled, turning back to fasten her seatbelt.

When her seatbelt was fastened, he eased the brake off and began moving the large truck out of the cluster of tents and back along what was left of the road toward the gates to the base.

CJ looked around in awe at the blackened buildings and strewn rubble. A destroyed Xakul fighter lay in the middle of the road, and Domik picked his way around it. She watched as the cockpit came into view, the corpse of the soldier who had flown the craft slumped over the controls.

She shuddered and looked away. "So, where are we going?"

"Oren heard of a tub near here that was grateful to the Taurean military for protecting it from Xakul attack."

"A what?"

"A tub? Isn't that what you call a place that has guests and helps them relax?" He shot her a confused look.

"I think you mean a spa."

Domik nodded. "That's right. A spa. Isn't that what I said?"

"No, a tub is... never mind. So we're going to a spa resort?"

He smiled at her, looking very pleased with himself. "Yes."

"Alone?"

"Is that ok?"

"It's perfect." She smiled.

The drive back to the gates took longer than the drive in. The road had been blasted in places with plasma charges and there was more than one fallen Xakul ship to pick their way around.

This time, when they made it to the gates, they were allowed to pass with no resistance. Domik turned the truck onto the highway and stretched his hand across the console to take CJ's in his.

"Krystal found some clothes for you." He tilted his head toward the back seat where a large duffle was sitting.

CJ closed her eyes and rested her head back against the headrest of the truck.

It was over. It was really over.

And she had a few days to spend with Domik.

Alone.

Together.

She shivered with anticipation of what the next few days might bring.

"You were going to tell me something?" She turned her head on the headrest to look at him through tired eyes.

He shot a glance at her and smiled. "Nothing that can't wait until we get there."

"All right," she said, closing her eyes. "I might just have a nap."

She let the noise of the engine and Domik's thumb stroking her hand lull her to sleep.

S he woke to the sound of the truck's tires on gravel and rubbed at her eyes. The headlights lit the road in front of them and, as Domik turned the vehicle, the lights illuminated a low brick building, its walls whitewashed. He stopped the truck and turned off the engine, the interior lights switching on and making CJ blink to clear her vision. Soft lights in the garden cast a warm glow over the terracotta stone of a series of paths around the building, giving the place a welcoming feel.

"Are we there?" CJ asked, sitting up from where she was slumped against the window and stretching her arms as far overhead as the truck would allow.

"We are," Domik said. He stopped the truck, turning off the engine and hopping out.

CJ opened her door, but he was right there, opening it and handing her down. "Are we far from the base?" She asked, watching as Domik opened the rear door and pulled out the duffel.

"Not that far, only an hour."

She followed him across the neatly swept stone path to the large wooden front door, which he opened, standing back to let her enter before him. She took her dusty boots off, setting them to one side of the door on a rack for that purpose, and wriggled her toes against the cool marble tiles. A lamp had been left lit, sending warm light spilling across the entry that opened into a large open-plan living area.

Domik shut the door behind them, locking it with a soft click. She spun on her heel to watch as he dropped the duffel bag to the floor and placed his own boots next to hers.

She stared at the two pairs of boots, the simple domesticity of his larger pair sitting next to hers sending a warmth through her chest. She lifted a hand to rub at her sternum.

"Clodagh?" Domik's deep voice rumbled near her ear and she started.

"Shit. Sorry, I'm still half asleep." She forced a smile as she turned to face him.

His brows drew together as he gave her a long look before handing her an envelope. "This was on the table." He tilted his head toward a small wooden table to one side of the entryway that she had overlooked. "Can you read it?"

"Sure," she said, taking the envelope and running her fingers over the thick paper. Their names were written in a curling script on the front, and she blinked rapidly to clear her stinging eyes.

Our names on a letter.

She opened it, pulling out a note welcoming them and providing keys for their stay. She read the contents aloud, then turned to Domik with a laugh. "This is definitely not a dodgy sex motel."

Domik snorted. He bent to pick up the duffel before heading further into the suite, CJ padding after him on her stockinged feet.

The marble tiles continued into a kitchen with a large matching pale gray marble island bench. As she moved closer, she spotted a bottle of wine in an ice bucket and a covered tray, and her stomach rumbled. The other half of the living area was carpeted, the soft cream color offsetting the terracotta of the walls. But it was the wall of glass that overlooked a wooden deck and the dark desert beyond that drew her.

CJ slid open one of the glass doors and stepped out onto the deck. "Wow," she breathed, tilting her head back to stare at the stars that shone bright in the darkness. "It's different when you know what's out there."

Domik followed her onto the deck.

CJ shot a glance over her shoulder, then gestured across the desert. "This place is something else." She crossed her arms over her chest and turned to face the huge alien warrior who had got under her skin so deep she never thought he would leave. "Tell me why we're here, Domik," she asked.

He looked down at his feet, shifting from foot to foot before meeting her eyes. He wasn't smiling, not that she expected him to be, but he had become a lot easier in her presence in the past few days, so the difference was abrupt.

Why is he nervous?

She waited, biting her lip to prevent filling in the silence.

I want to know. I have to know. What does he want from me?

He looked down at their hands, not meeting her eyes. "I want so many things, and I hope you want them, too."

"What do you want?" She reached to cup his jaw and turned his face, so he was looking at her.

"You said what happened at that motel was a one-time thing," he said, the words rough as if he was forcing himself to say them. His eyes were anguished. "Clodagh, I hope you want more from me. More than just..."

"A quick fuck?" She offered, hating the words as she said them.

He flinched. "If that's all you want from me, then I'll leave now. I'll walk back to the base. It will tear me apart, but you'll never have to see me again."

Her mouth had dropped open as he spoke. Her heart warmed as she dared to hope. "That's not what I want. It's not what I need."

He took a step closer to her, reaching out with a shaky hand to grip her fingers in his. "It isn't?"

"No. It isn't. I want much more." She smiled as she looked down at their hands, her much smaller fingers swallowed in his giant palm, but the way he held her was so gentle.

I am safe with Domik.

"I'm afraid," he said, and she couldn't have been more shocked if he had told her he was part octopus.

"You?" Her eyebrows had joined her hairline and she shook her head. "But you're not afraid of anything."

He chuckled, rubbing the back of his neck. "Not true."

She took a step closer but stuffed her hands in her pockets to stop from reaching for him. "What are you afraid of, Domik?"

A thick silence fell between them before he spoke, his words low and quiet. "I'm afraid of telling you how I feel and you not feeling the same way. I fear being hurt. But most of all, I'm terrified of not telling you how I feel and spending the rest of my life alone, filled with regret."

Her heart pounded in her chest as she stared up at him, eyes wide. The intensity of his gaze had her riveted to the spot. She could not have moved if she tried.

"You are my heart, Clodagh. You are the blood that pounds through my veins, the air that fills my lungs. Every waking thought and dream is of you. I exist because of you."

She blinked. Once, twice. Her eyes stung and then she couldn't blink fast enough to stop the tears that welled there. "Oh."

He cradled her face in his hands, his thumbs catching the tears that fell and brushing them gently away. "Say something, please."

She smiled a watery smile. "You love me." The certainty of the statement filled her, a warmth unlike anything she had ever felt, making her heart swell.

"Yes. With everything I am." A small smile lifted his lips before dropping, his usual stoic expression shuttering into place. "And now I've told you. If you don't think you can return my—"

"No!" she cried, throwing her arms around his neck and pressing kisses to every bit of exposed skin she could find.

"You don't love me?"

She laughed, pulling back so hazel eyes met brown. "No, silly. I love you more than anything. More than everything, on this planet and beyond. You just gave me a bit of a shock. Still waters run deep and all that."

"I don't understand," he said, his brows knitting.

She laughed again, sliding her arms around his waist and breathing in the scent of sweat and plasma and that unique scent that was all Domik. "Never mind. It's a human expression." He lifted her in his arms, and she squeaked. "What are you doing?"

"We are both filthy. Let's get clean."

She waggled her eyebrows at him. "And then we can get dirty?"

He threw his head back and let the most joyful laugh spill

into the night. "Yes, my little sunbeam. I will show you just how dirty I can get."

CJ giggled as he hefted her over one shoulder with ease, one arm clamped over the backs of her thighs to hold her in place. She tilted her head to watch, upside down, as he made his way down the hallway, through a bedroom with the biggest bed she had ever seen in her life, and then into a large ensuite bathroom.

He placed her gently on the edge of a bench between twin basins, his hips between her spread legs. His hands resting on either side of her hips, his large chest blocking most of the bathroom from her sight. Not that she wanted to look at anything but him. This massive, powerful man—alien—who was hers.

Mine.

The intensity of the thought was savage, and she grabbed the fabric of his shirt, pulling him toward her and lifting her face for his kiss.

Their lips met with more passion than finesse, hungry for each other with delving tongues and little nips that had her gasping. Domik pulled back, and she clung to him with a whimper, but he silenced her with a quick press of his lips to hers, before pulling off his shirt and tossing it over his shoulder.

She drank him in. All dark bronzed muscles and dark hair. His long black hair had escaped the braid and was spilling over his shoulders, and she reached up to finger a strand. "It's so soft." She smoothed the silken strands in wonder, loosening his remaining hair from the braid and running her hands over his scalp.

He groaned, dropping his head to her shoulder and

closing his eyes. "That feels so good."

She smiled, pulling her hands out of his hair. "I'll braid it for you if you like?"

"You will?" The look of boyish wonder on his face had her chuckling.

"I might not like long hair for myself, but it wasn't always this short."

"I'd like that."

He stepped back from the bench and undid the snap at the waistband of his pants. CJ was transfixed as he ran a hand over his taught stomach before shucking the combat trousers and standing in front of her naked.

"You don't wear underwear?" She choked out; eyes transfixed by the sheer heft of the cock that hung semi-hard between his legs.

He lifted an eyebrow and smirked.

CJ slid from the bench and quickly pulled her own clothes off until she was standing naked in front of him. She went to cross her hands over his chest, but stopped when he gave a short growl of protest.

"You are beautiful." He stepped closer to her, trailing a finger down her neck and between her breasts, her nipples peaking as goosebumps spread across her chest. Domik bent to take one nipple in his mouth and she gasped, her legs wobbling at the sensation that spread through her body. He gave the other the same attention, her wet flesh pebbling even more as the night air brushed over her.

He grinned and turned away to lean over the largest spa bath she had ever seen. How had she missed that?

Probably staring at Dom.

Like she was now, his taught ass in front of her as he

turned on the taps on the tub. Her hands moved of their own accord to grab the firm muscle and he jerked, looking over his shoulder.

"I like your ass," she said by way of an apology, giving one cheek a light smack. He straightened and turned to pick her up with a stern look she didn't believe for one second.

Her legs wrapped around his waist, and his thick length nudged against her center.

"Oh, I will not let that go," he bit out against her neck, nipping the sensitive skin below her ear.

She laughed, not worried in the least. He could crush her in one hand, and yet she knew he never would. She was the safest she had ever been, right here. In his arms. She sighed and let her head fall back, exposing her neck to his nibbles and kisses.

While the bath filled, Domik went back to the kitchen to get the wine, and CJ rummaged in the cupboard, finding a stash of bath bombs. A bright purple one gave her a chuckle, reminding her of that awful hotel and their first night together. She dropped it in the spa, smiling in amusement at the thought of Domik's giant body sprawling in the colored water.

But when he returned and stepped into the bath, she was far from laughing. The contrast of his bulging muscles and the pink water was more than her poor pussy could take, and she almost melted on the spot.

She slid into the bath, amazed that not only could they both fit, but she could face him comfortably, and reached for the glass of what she suspected was quite expensive bubbly wine that Domik passed her.

She slid deeper into the warm water with a sigh, the

liquid heat easing the aches of the past few days. She closed her eyes and rested her head against the side of the spa bath. Big hands gripped her around the middle, and she yelped with fright as she was lifted and placed bodily on Domik's lap.

She wriggled, and his cock thickened under her backside. She bit her lip as she watched him.

"What do you have in mind, Dom?" she asked, waggling her eyebrows suggestively.

She attempted to move on his lap, but he snaked an arm around her middle, holding her tightly as water and foam sloshed over the side of the bath.

One large arm wrapped around her waist held her against his chest, his lips brushing against her ear. The heat of his body seeped into her, the warm water lapping against her skin combining to make her muscles relax.

She was safe now. She had never felt safer in her life than she did right now.

In Domik's arms.

He passed her one of the glasses, and she lifted it to his. "To a long life together," she said as she tapped her glass against his.

"Yes," he said with a small smile, that dimple that teased her so peeking out to show itself.

She took a long pull of the wine; the bubbles bursting on her tongue. Moaning, she savored the feel and let her head fall back against Domik's chest.

He settled back, and she slid between his legs, his knees on either side of her and his strong thighs caging her in. She rested her arms on his legs and traced her fingers over his skin.

He put his glass down and reached for the bottle of shampoo to one side, squeezing some into his hand and lathering her scalp. She moaned at the feel of his hands as they massaged her head.

"That feels so good."

A wicked chuckle tickled her ear. "Just wait until I get you into that bed. Then I'll really make you feel good."

She laughed, feeling lighter than she had in months. No, years.

Warning her to keep her eyes shut, he lifted his hands and poured water over her scalp to rinse the shampoo from her hair.

He took a cloth and squeezed body wash onto it, then gently brushed it over the back of her neck, slowly sliding down to her shoulders and along her arms to her fingers. Goosebumps followed in the wake of his hand, and she swayed back, leaning against him with her eyes closed as he took her hand in his.

He washed every part of her so gently she wouldn't have believed he was capable of it if she hadn't witnessed it herself.

When he was done, she stood, the water around her calves, and turned to look down at him. Her breath caught as her eyes trailed over his bronzed skin, the bubbles from the bath decorating his chest. His hair was wet, and he lifted a hand to push it back from his face. The muscles in his arms bunched as he did, and CJ couldn't have stopped the groan that slipped from her lips if she'd tried.

"My turn," she said with a cheeky grin.

CHAPTER TWENTY-THREE

Domik

He watched as CJ slowly lowered herself to her knees in front of him, holding her hand out for the cloth. His eyes were fiery as he passed her the cloth. She only reached halfway down his chest before he gripped her wrist in his hand.

"Stop," he said.

Her brows knitted. "Why?"

He closed his eyes. "Your hands on me drive me to distraction."

She smiled, letting him take the cloth and watching as he rapidly finished what she had started, before he bundled her in a towel and carried her into the bedroom.

When he reached the bed, he released her slowly, her towel-clad body sliding down his. He caught the towel in one large hand and tugged it away from her, baring her body to his heated gaze. He lifted a hand to cup her cheek, and she smiled.

He bent his head to hers, resting his forehead against her own, and took a shaky breath. "I want to make this good for you."

"As long as you are touching me, it *will* be good, Dom," she said, leaning her head into his and wrapping her arms around his neck.

She tugged, standing on her toes so her lips met his. He shuddered at the brush of her lips, and CJ felt more powerful in that moment than she had ever before.

She pulled away, taking one of his hands in hers. Domik let her pull him toward the bed, unbelieving that he was really here. With her. About to do this.

And it was more than his poor, bitter heart could handle. He felt as if he would burst with all the words he wanted to say, but he just didn't know how to put all his feelings into words.

Then show her how you feel.

He watched as CJ took a jump and landed on the middle of the bed on her knees, her backside jiggling as she landed. She flopped onto her stomach with a laugh and rolled over onto her back; the covers twisting around her like a halo.

She lifted a hand and gestured for him to join her. As if a string was tied between them, he crossed the short distance to the bed and slid onto it next to her. His weight made the mattress dip, and she rolled into him.

"Well," she said with a laugh, "that's one way to get me close to you."

Domik could no longer hold back, and he reached for her waist, lifting her to straddle his hips. He slid backward until his back hit the mass of pillows piled up against the headboard and settled against them, half sitting and half lying down.

His hands wrapped around her waist, thumbs touching just under her bellybutton, fingertips brushing together at her back. His thumbs moved on the soft skin of her belly, sliding up and down against the slight give.

Her thighs were parted over him, and his eyes were drawn to the center of her, covered by a patch of neatly trimmed dark hair. He dropped his hands to the top of her thighs and dipped his thumbs between her legs, tracing up and down those soft curls, gently stroking.

His cock hardened, almost painfully thick, pulsing with the blood that rushed to his groin. He felt it throbbing with the need to be inside her. To delve into her tight, wet heat and find the peace he knew would be waiting.

He dragged his eyes away from what tempted him the most, taking in her rapidly rising and falling chest. Her breasts were high and small, topped with rosy red nipples that bunched into tight little peaks.

He tugged her forward, but she resisted, her hands on his chest, her small fingers tracing patterns on his skin. She looked up at him from under her lashes and smiled shyly.

"I love you, Domik," she said.

He nodded, again trying to tug her forward, but she laughed and he let go.

"Aren't you going to say something?" She lifted an eyebrow, but her expression wasn't one of anger.

Domik sighed, dropping his head back against the headboard of the bed. "What do you want me to say?"

She lifted a hand to tap him lightly on the tip of his nose. "Whatever you feel, Dom." She leaned forward to drop a kiss on his lips, so lightly he wasn't sure if he'd imagined it. "I want to know how you feel."

He gave her a flat look.

"And don't scowl me out of asking. That doesn't work on me, and you know it." She shook her finger at him, and he grabbed her wrist, pulling her hand to his lips and kissing each of her fingers. "And don't weasel out of this by using your mouth in other ways."

He groaned, but let her hand go. "All right. You win."

She grinned, flopping to one side and lying on her stomach, her face resting on her hands. "Go on."

If he was going to do this, he had to be touching her. So he reached across and pulled her close to his side. She squeaked, but didn't resist.

"Clodagh, I am no good with words." He lifted a finger to shush her when she protested. "But for you, I will try."

He was rewarded with a brilliant smile that filled him with warmth.

You lied. For her, you would do anything. Tell her that.

He licked his lips and watched her for a few moments before continuing. "I don't say how I feel because there are not enough words for me to express how deep my feelings for you go. I could fill oceans with my need to see you smile. All the stars in the universe pale compared to how beautiful you are. My heart beats only for you. My cock throbs only for you. Every morning when I wake, my first thoughts are of you, and when I go to sleep and close my eyes, it is your face I see. You haunt my dreams, Clodagh." He swallowed past a lump that formed in his throat. "A life without you in it is not a life I wish to imagine."

As he spoke, she had sat up, arms crossed over her chest

and one hand covering her mouth. A single tear leaked from one eye and snaked its way down her cheek. Seeing it, Domik reached for her and smoothed his thumb across it, wiping it away.

"Don't cry, my heart. I never want to see you sad." His voice was a deep rumble in the quiet room.

She smiled a shaky smile. "I'm not crying because I'm sad."

"You're not?"

"No. I'm crying because I'm happy."

He must have looked as surprised as he felt because she laughed.

"I love you, Domik. Every day, I love you more and more. I've loved you for so long that it's a part of who I am. I don't want a life without you in it, either."

She crawled over to him on her knees and straddled his lap once more. "And I am really tuned on by all this talk." She leaned forward to brush her nose over his.

Domik smiled and pulled her closer to meet his lips, nipping lightly against her bottom lip as she melted against him. He wrapped one arm around her middle, tugging her against him, the other sliding up her back to cradle her head and arrange her just how he wanted.

He pulled back, watching her with dark eyes filled with passion. "What you make me feel..." He growled as he bent her backward over his arm and lifted her breast to his lips. She was so small in his arms, so slight compared to how big he was, that he was afraid of hurting her. "I don't want to hurt you," he said, as he moved from one breast to the other.

"Don't be gentle," she said, a hard edge to her voice. "I am sick to death of feeling fragile. I want you to be yourself with me," she said. "Besides, I don't think you could hurt me. You'd hurt yourself well before you would do anything to hurt me. I'm yours, Domik. Show me how I make you feel."

With her last words, he gathered her close to him and rolled them both over on the bed, tucking her underneath him and settling his hips between her thighs.

She laughed, sliding her arms around his neck and lifting her head to meet his lips. They crashed together, hard kisses softening into teasing nibbles as they explored each other. Her hands drifted down his shoulders, and he shivered as she slid them down his chest to tweak his nipples.

"Oh, I'll remember that you like that," she said, and he smothered her words with more kisses, sliding down her body to cup her breasts with his hands, thumbs slipping over their hardened peaks in a rhythm that had her squirming. She arched her back, and he took that as a sign to continue his exploration, drifting kisses down her stomach until he reached those dark, silky curls once more.

Wasting no time, he dipped his tongue through the center of her and she cried out, grasping his hair in her hands and pulling him closer. He grinned against her wetness as he slid his hands beneath her buttocks, spreading her open for him to feast upon her flesh. "That's it, little one. Open for me." He licked her in a long, leisurely pass that had her back arching as she gasped with pleasure. "That's it, just like that. Just feel."

Her hands tightened in his hair, the little bite of pain sending shooting pleasure down his spine so that he almost spilled against the sheets. He pushed his hips into the bed, attempting to squash the need to be inside her. "If you do that again, I won't be able to wait," he said, then growled in warning.

I need to get inside her, but not before she finds her pleasure.

She went to grab at his hair again, and he released her hips to grab her wrists in one of his big hands. CJ giggled, which quickly broke off as he slid one thick finger inside her, curling it to find the spot that sent her wild. She clenched against him, gasping as he licked and sucked the little bundle of nerves at the apex of her core. He added another finger, gently easing her open, and she spasmed around him. Her little gasps and cries as she came apart making him growl with satisfaction.

He pushed her through her release until she wriggled her hands to get free. He pulled away, looking up at her from between her spread thighs. Her eyes were glazed as she looked at him with a lazy smile. He wiped his face on the back of his hand and crawled up the bed over her, his hips settling onto hers to press her into the mattress, his heavy cock trapped between their stomachs. He moved his hips slowly, grinding the length of him through her wet folds. She lifted her hips and pushed back, gasping as he shifted his hips.

"I need you, Dom. Now." She grabbed at his shoulders with desperate fingers.

"Be patient, little sun." He smiled, and she closed her eyes with a sigh, dropping her head back against the pillow.

He reached back to lift one of her legs and place is on his shoulder, looking down at his cock next to her center. She wriggled, and he gripped her hip in one hand to hold her still. "I'm big, Clodagh. Hold still, I don't want to hurt you."

"I have a better idea," she said, gesturing for him to move off her.

He let her move him onto his back, his legs over the side

of the bed and his feet flat on the ground. He lifted up on his elbows to watch as she climbed onto his lap. Her thighs spread over his lap, and she lifted a hand to his shoulder to steady herself as she reached between them to fist his cock in her other hand. "Are you ready?" she asked with a teasing wink.

"Yes," he croaked.

She lowered herself onto him, and the sight of her body gripping him as she eased her slick downwards was almost enough to have him explode. He gritted his teeth and kept still as she settled onto his lap as far as she could take him.

"Fuck, you're so thick." She moaned, head thrown back and her eyes closed. She lifted a little and eased herself down again, both of them crying out as pleasure shot through them. He lost all sense of time as she lifted up and down, taking him a little deeper each time until she sat fully on his lap, his cock entirely sheathed within her.

"Domik?" she panted, barely audible.

"Yes?" He sat up, sliding one hand around her to her close to him, his palm between her shoulder blades. His other hand slid between them to tease her clit.

"Oh, fuck! You feel so good," she cried out.

"Play with yourself," he demanded and smiled when she obeyed without question, sliding her much smaller hand between them to strum her clit.

He pulled his hand free and rested it on her hip before giving an experimental thrust up into her. She moaned, her short nails biting into his shoulder. He felt her hand between them moving over herself, brushing against the base of his cock as he slid partway out, before sliding back home.

His chest felt like it would explode, his heart was so full.

"You are the light of the dawn, the first flowers in spring," he said against her hair.

She looked up at him, her eyes sparkling and her mouth falling open in an o as she tightened around him.

"My heart is yours, Clodagh," he said, his voice rough.

"I love you, Dom," she said, throwing her head back and gasping as she gave a little cry of pleasure.

"That's it, little sun. Let go. I'll always be here to catch you. You and me. Always."

As if his words had freed her, she shattered around him, Domik following her to his own climax. Panting, he flopped backward on the bed and slid from her body. He tucked her against his chest and smiled down at the woman who meant so much to him.

She laughed, pushing a sweat-slicked lock of hair back from his forehead. "So, what now?"

He smiled, lifting a hand to her cheek. "Now we live our life."

EPILOGUE

CJ

O *ne year later*

CJ shifted from foot to foot, nervous energy shooting through her as she stared at the blank view screen mounted on the wall. In an hour, it would all be over.

Please let it be over. Finally.

She ran a hand over her head, mussing the blond pixie cut that she still wore, and turned her back on the viewscreen to pace. Back and forth, she walked over the thick cream-colored living room carpet in the home she shared with Domik. They had only moved in a few weeks before.

The dwelling was modest, but it had a yard big enough for a dog. When she had expressed the desire to have a pet, Domik had promptly brought home a squirming greyhound puppy, and she had immediately fallen in love. She had named the puppy Marsh, short for marshmallow, as one pleading look from his enormous eyes had Domik turn as soft as the sugary treat. CJ had found the two of them sprawled out on the large couch in the living room many times, much to her amusement.

The sound of the front door opening had CJ turning to see Domik walk inside, her breath catching at the sight of him still after all this time. His hair was neatly braided, falling past his broad shoulders. He was wearing a tight-fitting tee-shirt that clung appealingly to his chest and arms. He had taken to wearing jeans when he wasn't at work, and as he turned to usher the dog inside, CJ admired his firm backside.

CJ bent to greet Marsh, who trotted up to her with his usual bouncy gait and pressed his face forward for a scratch behind the ears. She dropped to her knees and sighed, burying her face in the dog's neck.

"Everything all right?" Domik asked.

CJ broke away, letting the now squirming dog go to rush over to his bed in the room's corner and settle in, watching with gigantic eyes.

"Yes... no. I don't know." She stood, throwing her hands up in exasperation. "It's just been so long and I want it to be over."

"It will. Come here," he said, crossing the space between her in long strides and gathering her to his chest.

She sighed, closing her eyes as a calm spread through her. In the months since the Xakul attack on Earth, a lot had changed. The main Xakul attack had been dealt with quickly, but some soldiers had landed and gone to ground. A combined force of human and Taurean troops had hunted them down, one by one, until the Xakul no longer posed a threat to Earth. That had taken months.

Domik had accepted a position on Taurus, not working

with weaponry but in medical technology. He'd decided that he was more interested in helping people and now led a team of engineers who were refining the midi-scanning technology to better suit other races. CJ had accompanied him and now worked in a clinic on Taurus alongside Amelia. The clinic had become the place to seek medical treatment for the many humans who now lived on the planet as part of increased Taurean-human relations.

T'arq and Krystal were now working to upgrade and test various cloaking technologies for the Taurean military. The last time they spoke, Krystal told CJ that she was interested in making the teleporting technology more accurate. CJ knew there would be news about that sometime soon.

That left Zac, Laila, and Oren, who were kept busy hunting down Taurean Purists. The Taureans had quickly identified the splinter group that had instigated the attack on the Taurean fleet and delayed their arrival at Earth, and they had been found guilty of treason. The trial had been conducted on Taurus, concluding a few months earlier, and the convicted were sent to Garveli V, a prison planet on the outskirts of Taurean space.

Dealing with the human "resistance" had taken a little longer. There had been no laws on Earth that considered aliens and extraterrestrial politics, so it had been one hell of a mess. But today, finally, the verdict would be delivered.

CJ lifted her head and met his lips with hers briefly before pulling away to give him a small smile. "I just worry that they won't be found guilty."

"Why don't you sit down? It won't be long until they get started. Want a coffee?" Domik waved at the low couch that took up most of the space in front of the viewscreen.

"Thank you," CJ said. She sat on the couch, kicking off her shoes and tucking her feet underneath her.

He smoothed a hand over her hair and smiled, that dimple that had teased her so many months ago making an appearance. "It's going to be fine."

Yes, it really will be.

Marsh jumped up from his bed and bounded over to join her on the couch, curling up next to her and putting his head in her lap. CJ smiled and patted his slick coat.

Domik walked back into the room with two cups of coffee in time to see the view screen that took up almost the entire far well flicker into life. He sat on the couch next to CJ, the dog on the other side of her, and draped an arm over her shoulders.

It had taken months to track down all the offenders. The human resistance fighters had been much easier to find than the Taurean Purists. Many of the Purists had gone to ground on the outer reach planets. The humans had to be tried on Earth in a court of their peers. The Taureans had to be tried on Taurus.

CJ and Domik had both been required to give evidence, as had many of the team. Oren figured prominently, as he had been key in interrupting the Purist's attempts to disrupt the attack on the Taurean fleet.

And today, the humans would have the verdict passed down. The viewscreen crackled into life, a man in a suit holding a microphone appeared.

"Good afternoon, ladies and gentlemen. Today, we will hear the verdict of the human resistance fighters." The crowd behind the man jostled him slightly, and he took a step slightly off camera. "As you can see, the crowd today is a little agitated."

CJ turned to Dominic with a wry smile. "I wonder why they're agitated?"

The camera zoomed to a man who appeared at the top of the broad set of stairs, the crowd below him jostling backward and forth, only held back by security guards. CJ squinted, realizing that this was General Russell, this time looking a little more put together than the time she had seen him after the Xakul attack on Earth. The general held his arms up and was facing the crowd, seeking silence.

"The verdict has been delivered on the resistance fighters. The jury has found them..." He waited until the crowd was silent. CJ rolled her eyes at the dramatics. "The jury has found them guilty."

A hush spread over the crowd before a single voice shouted, "how will they be punished?"

The general ignored the question, and the murmurs from the crowd that followed. He turned and walked back inside the building.

The journalist with the microphone appeared on camera again. His face was now pale. "The resistance fighters have been declared guilty." He looked down at a crumpled piece of paper in his hand and swallowed before staring back into the camera. "They are to be sent off-planet to the Taurean prison planet of Garveli V, the same prison planet where the Taurean Purists were sentenced earlier this year."

"I suppose that's that then," she said, turning away as the man on the view screen began interviewing a member of the crowd, who was waving a placard angrily. She lifted the remote and switched the view screen off. "It's over." She closed her eyes and huffed out a sigh.

"Are you OK?" Domik asked, his dark eyes concerned.

She looked up at him. "Yes, with you by my side, I can do anything."

Domik took her hands in his and smoothed his thumbs over her fingers. "I want to spend my life with you. To go where you go. To share in your joys and your sorrows." He slid off the couch to drop to one knee.

She gaped at him.

He gave a shaky smile. "I want you to be my mate in the Taurean fashion, and I want to be your husband in the human tradition."

"You're asking me to marry you?" she asked.

"Yes, I'm asking you to marry me."

She smiled at him before answering. "No."

Domik's expression was stricken as he stared at her, his mouth falling open. "Oh, I misunderstood—"

"No, you didn't. Let me explain." She took his hands and dipped her head to meet his eyes. "There's nothing for me on Earth. I have never wanted to get married. But to join with you in the Taurean tradition? Yes. That I would very much like."

He blinked. "You will be my mate?"

"Yes, I will be your mate." She leaned forward and kissed him.

Domik surged to his feet, gripping CJ by the waist and hoisting her over his shoulder so quickly she let out a surprised shriek.

"Domik!"

He clamped a hand over her legs and strode from the

room, CJ giggling. He pushed open their bedroom door and strode toward the bed before lowering her to her feet.

"I love you, Clodagh," he said, his voice deep with emotion.

"I love you too, big guy," she said, lifting onto her toes to meet his lips.

He crushed her to him, and she reveled in the strength in his arms.

She was safe.

She was loved.

She was home.

The End

———

Thank you for reading *Alien Domination*!
I would really appreciate you rating my book or leaving an honest review.

If you want to keep up to date with my writing you can sign up for my newsletter via my website
www.melodybeckett.com/newsletter

Alien Domination is the third Taurean Warriors book, and it ties off the 'save Earth' plot that started in the prequel, *Alien Attraction*.

Haven't read the prequel yet?
Read on to find out more...

ALIEN ATTRACTION
SHE DOESN'T BELIEVE ALIENS EXIST... UNTIL ONE NEEDS HER HELP.

Commander Oren Ka'Ress is having a bad day. First he crash lands on a primitive planet and is injured in the crash, then he—and his dangerous Xakul prisoner—are captured. Oren needs backup, but with no way to contact his fellow Taureans, he's stuck.

Dr. Amelia O'Malley doesn't believe in aliens... until a mysterious patient arrives on her ward. Bigger than any man she's ever seen, and with inhumanly bright eyes, Amelia finds herself full of questions. But there's one problem—Amelia can't understand anything he says.

As the Xakul threat looms, Oren must find a way for Amelia to understand him. With the clock counting down there is more at stake than either of them could dream...

———

Download your FREE eBook when you join Melody's newsletter.

www.melodybeckett.com/newsletter

ACKNOWLEDGMENTS

Writing a book is hard work. Revising a book is harder, or at least it is for me. My proof reader is my husband, Mr B, and is worth his weight in gold for the attention to detail he shows, and the many arguments about whether a character would or would not say or do a certain thing. Thank you, you wonderful human. I'm taking you out to dinner to say thanks.

My editor, Tiffany of Write Now Creative, does a fantastic job of not pulling her punches, something I am incredibly thankful for.

It's the friendship of great women that I will always be thankful for. Caity, Britt, Liz, Kellie. You are all awesome. Thanks for reading my books and supporting my work.

And, as always, thank you to you. My reader. I am so very thankful that you took a chance on this book. :)

Happy reading!

Mel xx

ABOUT THE AUTHOR

Melody has been a voracious reader of anything with a happy ending since she was old enough to pick up a book. As a teenager she pulled all-nighters reading romance novels under the covers with a torch. She still reads like a fiend, and can always be found with her e-reader within reach!

As a writer, she pens the stories her teenage self wished existed: stories that marry her love for science fiction, action movies, and romance, and stories with happy ever afters.

She hopes you enjoy reading them as much as she enjoys writing them for you!

To keep up to date with Melody's writing and for special offers, sign up to her newsletter.

www.melodybeckett.com/newsletter

ALSO BY MELODY BECKETT

Taurean Warriors Series

Alien Attraction

Alien Desire

Alien Seduction

Alien Domination

Other works

An Alien for Christmas